Blaze™

Alaska—the last frontier.

*The nights are long. The days are cold.
And the men are really, really HOT!*

*Can you think of a better excuse
for a trip up north?*

Don't miss the chance to experience some

Alaskan Heat

Jennifer LaBrecque's new sizzling miniseries:

Northern Exposure
(October 2010)

Northern Encounter
(November 2010)

Northern Escape
(December 2010)

Enjoy the adventure!

Blaze

Dear Reader,

Once in a lifetime, you discover a place that touches something inside you. Alaska was one of those places for me. At the time I had never seen such wild, unspoiled beauty, or a landscape that varied from barren to the lushness of the Matanuska Valley to the magnificence of millennia-old glaciers. And the state is inhabited by some of the most interesting people you'll ever meet.

Obviously, I fell in love with Alaska.

And when the opportunity came along to create my own Alaskan paradise, I was thrilled. I totally enjoyed bringing Good Riddance—a small town in the Alaskan bush, where you can leave behind whatever troubles you—to life! Founded by a transplanted Southern belle, Good Riddance is home to a quirky assortment of folks from all walks of life. It's the perfect place to fall in love.

So welcome to Good Riddance. I hope you enjoy your stay. And don't forget to drop by and visit me at www.jenniferlabrecque.com.

As always...happy reading,

Jen

Jennifer LaBrecque

NORTHERN EXPOSURE

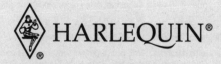

TORONTO • NEW YORK • LONDON
AMSTERDAM • PARIS • SYDNEY • HAMBURG
STOCKHOLM • ATHENS • TOKYO • MILAN • MADRID
PRAGUE • WARSAW • BUDAPEST • AUCKLAND

Recycling programs
for this product may
not exist in your area.

ISBN-13: 978-0-373-79574-1

NORTHERN EXPOSURE

Copyright © 2010 by Jennifer LaBrecque

www.eHarlequin.com

Printed in U.S.A.

ABOUT THE AUTHOR

After a varied career path that included barbecue-joint waitress, corporate number cruncher and bug-business maven, Jennifer LaBrecque has found her true calling writing contemporary romance. Named 2001 Notable New Author of the Year and 2002 winner of the prestigious Maggie Award for Excellence, she is also a two-time RITA® Award finalist. Jennifer lives in suburban Atlanta.

Books by Jennifer LaBrecque

HARLEQUIN BLAZE

Don't miss any of our special offers. Write to us at the following address for information on our newest releases.

Harlequin Reader Service
U.S.: 3010 Walden Ave., P.O. Box 1325, Buffalo, NY 14269
Canadian: P.O. Box 609, Fort Erie, Ont. L2A 5X3

To the intrepid men and women
who settled the last frontier.

Acknowledgment

Thanks to Dr. Roger L. Swingle II,
for his patience with all of my questions
and his willingness to share his knowledge
and love of Alaska with me. Any inaccuracies
in the book are all my own.

You're the best, Rog.

Prologue

SOME DAYS, LADY LUCK was with you and on others, she didn't ever bother to show up. The way it was looking, she wouldn't be flying with him today.

Dalton Saunders, former corporate drone CPA, current Alaskan bush pilot, had planned to go fishing with Clint Sisnuket on this fine October day. Instead, he was going to spend his Sunday afternoon making an unscheduled run.

"You need for me to fly to Anchorage?"

Merrilee Danville Weatherspoon, transplanted Southern belle, mayor and founder of Good Riddance, Alaska, and proprietor of Good Riddance Air Strip Center and Bed and Breakfast, nodded. "Sorry, Dalton. The fish are going to have to bite without you today. Juliette was going to make it but she's got engine problems."

Juliette covered his days off and picked up the overflow runs, but if she was grounded, there wasn't much sense arguing. Not unless he wanted to come across like Jeb Taylor and Dwight Simmons, who sat in rocking chairs with the chess table between them. The grizzled old-timers never agreed on anything other than hanging out at the airstrip and dickering.

"Can't do much about engine problems," Dalton said. But damn, this was probably going to be one of the last nice days they'd have. It had been unseasonably warm for October today. For that matter, it'd been unseasonably warm period. The loons were still out at the lake and it was the latest they'd ever stayed in the years he'd been here. "What am I picking up?"

"Not what. Who. You're picking up a doctor who's filling in the next few weeks for Doc Morrow. Dr. Shanahan."

Dalton had flown Good Riddance's doctor, Barry Morrow, into Anchorage Friday evening for the first leg of his vacation. Dalton supposed it was only fitting that now he'd have to pick up Doc Morrow's replacement. Although it would have saved him a trip if this Dr. Shanahan had been ready to go on Friday.

Snagging a cup of coffee from the carafe on the small carved table next to the desk that housed all of the radio equipment, Dalton nodded. "Guess we're lucky to find a replacement."

Merrilee nodded. "Isn't that the truth?" Her smile crinkled the corners of her eyes. "And here I thought we'd be overwhelmed with doctors wanting to fill in for a few weeks in our fair city."

Dalton laughed as Merrilee intended. But actually, she was right. Very few visitors came through who weren't immediately charmed by Good Riddance. The town had been just what he'd been looking for eight years ago when he'd tossed in the towel on the rat race that was his life in Michigan.

Watching his father die, weeks from retirement from a job he despised, had changed Dalton's life. His dad had put off living until he retired and, ironically, he hadn't lived to enjoy it. Swearing he wouldn't make the same mistake, Dalton had unloaded his job, condo and fiancée and pursued what he really wanted—a job as a bush pilot in the Alaskan wilds.

Dalton and his dad had always shared a fascination with their country's last frontier. For Dalton's sixteenth birthday, he and his dad had spent four days on an Alaskan fishing trip. How many times since then had he and his dad talked about a "big" return trip to Alaska, once his dad retired, of course? Countless. Alaska had been their shared dream. Even though he and his father had never made that trip together, he'd felt closer to his dad in Good Riddance than he ever had in Michigan.

Good Riddance was a great place to leave a lot of things behind. He mentally shook off thoughts of Laura, his former fiancée. He'd considered himself damn lucky to have tossed in that particular towel—and that type of woman. Ambition, plain and simple, had been the nail in their relationship coffin. Laura's ambition had led her into bed with Dalton's boss, who apparently had the measure of ambition Laura found lacking in Dalton. Although it had hurt like a bitch at the time, he figured it'd been his lucky break in the long run.

So, if he occasionally missed a Sunday afternoon

fishing trip to haul in some relief doc for Merrilee, well, it still beat the hell out of the life he'd had before.

"Dr. Shanahan, huh?" he said.

"Yep. I've made you a sign and everything." Merrilee handed over a placard for him to hold up at the arrival area.

Finishing the last of his coffee, he traded the now-empty cup for the sign. "Alright then, I guess I'll go get our new doc."

He sighed as he headed out. Sure was a nice day. If the trip went fast, maybe he and Clint could still get a little fishing in. Heck, maybe they'd take the new doc with them.

1

As Dr. Skye Shanahan made her way off the plane in Anchorage she wondered again how she'd allowed herself to be railroaded into this Alaskan bush debacle. Guilt, plain and simple. Maternal manipulation, at its finest.

Skye was never quite allowed to forget that she was something of a disappointment to her parents. Sure, she carried the title of doctor but her mother, father and brother were neurosurgeons. And her sister had done the next best thing and married one. Nope, in a family of brilliance, Skye was a lowly general practitioner and still single to boot. Single, with the innate ability to pick the wrong guy. When her last boyfriend had left her with egg on her face, Skye had vowed to take a hiatus. Unfortunately, that left the door wide open for her mother and sister to step up to the matchmaking plate. And they were determined to hit a home run.

Skye had had neurosurgeons, orthopedists, even a podiatrist thrown at her to the point of ridiculousness.

So when Skye's mother and Barry Morrow's mother—Barry was the poor soul buried in some backwoods Alaska bush practice—put their heads together in some misguided attempt to get their children together, Skye had given in—on the condition that he'd be the last man they sent her way.

And that was precisely why she'd given up a sunny Caribbean vacation to squander two weeks in this God-forsaken place. She was a city girl, born and raised in Atlanta. She didn't do bush or outback or all of that other stuff—except now she apparently did.

Granted she'd been feeling an underlying restlessness for the last year or so. It was as if she'd been so caught up in med school and residency and then joining a practice that she hadn't thought any further. Once those things had been accomplished, she was almost disappointed. But that was ridiculous. How could she be discontent with her life? *Maybe because you're bored,* an insidious little voice whispered in her head.

But *if* she was bored, Alaska certainly wasn't the answer.

She tamped back a momentary panic at the thought of spending two weeks in Good Riddance, practicing what amounted to frontier medicine. What if she couldn't hack it? Then she squared her shoulders. She'd manage. Shanahans didn't fail—that simply wasn't an option.

She quickly found and stepped into the women's restroom. It had been a long flight. Although she knew it was quirky, she couldn't use the plane facilities. The claustrophobic nature of being in such a small, tight space and the incredibly irrational fear she carried from being on a plane the very first time as a six-year-old—when she'd thought that she'd be sucked out into the atmosphere when she'd flushed—made using the on-board facilities impossible.

She'd taken care of her business, washed her hands, tucked a stray hair back into her chignon and was touching up her lipstick when someone tapped her on the shoulder. Startled, she turned. A short woman of obvious native heritage stood next to Skye, a friendly smile on her face.

"Yes?"

"This is for you," the woman said, pressing something into Skye's hand.

"What…?" Instinctively she dropped the object and it clattered to the bathroom counter. It was a rock with the word "Yes" printed on it.

"It is yours now," the stranger said.

Why would Skye want a rock? The stranger continued, "I saw you and sensed your unrest. That's when I knew the rock belonged to you. Everything you need to know can be found in that rock. It is your answer rock."

Skye was a woman of science, of fact. But there was a part of her she seldom visited that embraced the fanciful notion of a flat stone carrying universal answers. She didn't particularly believe it but she liked the idea. And it was that fanciful part of her that led her to pick up the rock and curl her fingers around the smooth surface. "Thank you."

The woman turned to walk away and glanced back over her shoulder. "Welcome home."

Skye opened her mouth to tell the stranger that she wasn't from Alaska but the woman had already left. She dropped the stone into her purse along with her lipstick and hoisted her purse onto her shoulder. Even though it had been a strange encounter, there had been something strangely calming about it.

Exiting the washroom, she glanced around but the woman was nowhere to be seen. Funny. She'd known, somehow, that she wouldn't be.

Putting the strange encounter behind her, she focused on finding her ride to Good Riddance. She exited the area that was gated off for security purposes and scanned the people obviously awaiting arrivals. It took about two seconds to spot the broad-shouldered, dark-haired man holding a placard with her last name on it.

She had the craziest reaction as her eyes met his across the crowded room. It was cliché, tired and slightly insane but her breath caught and held in her throat as his gaze tangled with hers. Her legs were slightly unsteady as she crossed the remaining few feet. No, no and no. She was face-to-face with her worst nightmare. At an intellectual level, everything about him screamed Mr. Wrong. However, at a visceral, cellular level, everything inside her had flipped to "On." She shook her head. She hadn't flown across the damn country looking for some quiet space to regroup only to find herself face-to-face with the one kind of man she shouldn't want—an Alaskan sky cowboy.

"Hi, I'm Shanahan," she said.

Looking at possibly the sexiest man she'd ever laid eyes on, her heart lodged somewhere in her throat. She was tingling in all the wrong places…or right places, if she wasn't standing in the middle of Anchorage, Alaska's airport. Apparently she had a weakness for a rugged flannel-shirted man in need of a shave with dark hair curling past his collar. But no. She was *so* not going to make this mistake.

"You're the relief doc?" He sounded as startled as she felt. But now, she felt even more nonplussed because he sounded as yummy as he looked. And what the hell was wrong with her? Hadn't she vowed, promised herself no men who were all wrong for her? So, she could stand around like some goof or she could nip this right in the bud.

Besides, that *Doc* business irritated her to no end. And irritation was so much healthier for her in the long run than this surge of unwanted attraction that had roiled through her. *"Doctor—"* she stressed the entire word "—Skye Shanahan." She held out her hand. "Pleased to meet you…"

"Dalton Saunders," he said. His handshake was dry, firm, no-nonsense. A flummoxing jolt traveled through her. It wasn't static electricity, but was more like a shock to her entire central nervous system. She practically snatched her hand back.

"Nice to meet you, Dr. Shanahan." Dark, spiky lashes fringed his topaz eyes. "I'll be your pilot for the last leg of your trip to Good Riddance. I'll also be the one to take you out into the bush if there's an emergency."

There was no reason why the thought of being in a small plane with this man should make her heart pound, but it did. Not acceptable. He made her uncomfortable. She didn't want to spend the next two weeks with him acting as her chauffeur in the sky—although she'd been told it was unlikely she'd be making emergency bush visits. However, she supposed anything was possible.

"I thought bush pilots were older," she said, feeling stupid the moment the words left her mouth. And she didn't like feeling stupid.

He looked momentarily taken aback. Like a shift in the wind, his manner went from laid-back to stiff. "I assure you I'm very capable." For one second, just a fraction of time in space, there was a look, a gleam in his smoky golden eyes that literally had her toes curling inside her wedge heels. "I have an excellent record, Doc."

She was suddenly extremely warm underneath her silk and angora turtleneck and soft wool pantsuit. She actually felt slightly feverish. It certainly wouldn't do to get sick at this point in time. "I was simply expecting someone older," she said.

"So was I."

She looked every day of her twenty-nine years in her estimation but that still didn't look old enough to most patients. That was the reason she'd taken to wearing clear-lens black-rimmed glasses. In the end, her skills won patients over, but she'd learned long ago that the glasses, professional dress and a polished demeanor went a long way toward setting the stage and meeting expectations. She gave him her best quelling look. "I'm extremely competent."

Undaunted, and her look usually daunted the best of them, he grinned at her. "Backatcha...Doc."

She rubbed her index finger along her temple. That grin was lethal to a woman's resolve. "Sorry about that. I should know better. I've been fighting that particular battle since residency. It's tough to be taken seriously when you're a woman."

"I noticed, Dr. Shanahan," he said. And while there wasn't anything offensive in his words, there was a note of awareness in his voice that sent a whoosh of color up into her face. Very primal. Very elemental. Him, man. Her, woman.

"I apologize. I'm sure you're very competent," she said, falling back on her professionalism in an attempt to quell what felt like an intimate moment between two strangers.

He nodded, a faintly wicked glimmer in his eyes. "Of course I am. Otherwise I wouldn't be standing here."

Skye laughed. She got the implication—incompetent bush pilots were either grounded or six feet under.

An answering smile lit his eyes and for a moment she forgot to breathe. "So, is that your bag, Doc?" He nodded toward her carry-on. "We can head out."

He must be kidding. She always packed a carry-on bag with her toiletries and two changes of clothing and undergarments. That way if her suitcases got lost in transit, she wasn't stranded without anything. There was much to be said for not being caught unawares. But she was here for two weeks. Her carry-on bag would cover her for two days.

Apparently, however, he wasn't being funny. Mr. Saunders was already turning to go.

"No, this isn't everything. We'll need to pick them up at baggage claim."

"Them?" His dark eyebrows lowered.

"I never quite mastered the art of packing light." Not to mention she was about to be in the back country. It wasn't as if she could just run down the street to one of twenty stores to pick up whatever she needed out here in the cold, God-forsaken Alaskan wilderness. "You might want to grab a luggage cart."

"YOU KNOW MY PLANE HAS a weight limit," Dalton said as he stacked yet another matching bag, all in a green and blue paisley pattern, for crying out loud, on the cart. She'd brought a ton of stuff with her. You'd think she was checking into the Ritz Carlton instead of the Good Riddance Bed and Breakfast.

From the moment he saw her crossing the terminal, in her trim pantsuit, elegant hairstyle, and now the matching designer luggage, he knew she was the ambitious sort.

Was that a blush creeping its way up beneath her freckle-kissed porcelain skin? Nah. Probably just a flash of temper that went with that gorgeous red hair of hers. At least he suspected it would be gorgeous if it was tumbling down around her shoulders rather than pinned into an elegant twist at the nape of her neck.

His fingers itched to reach over and pluck a few pins and watch it fall and see just what color her eyes turned then. And that was just plain dumb-ass considering she was exactly the type of woman he needed to avoid.

She had the most incredibly amazing blue eyes. The name Skye didn't fit *her*—nah, she was Dr. Shanahan up one side and down the other—but it fit her *eyes* to a "T." They were the color of the sky Dalton flew through, which was a distinctly different shade than you saw when you were on the ground looking up. Yep, her eyes were the open sky at fair-weather flying altitude. Fringed by reddish-gold lashes that led him to believe her hair color was real and not out of a bottle. Of course there was one sure way to know and of its own volition his mind quickly sketched an image of her naked—red hair down around her shoulders, pale freckled skin with a thatch of fiery red curls at the apex of her thighs.

And damn it to hell, he had absolutely no business standing here daydreaming about the good doctor without clothes. Alaskan men had a reputation for being woman-desperate, but he was far from that. He hooked up occasionally with Janice, a cute diner waitress in Juneau, and outside of that, rounding up a date now and then wasn't difficult. No, he wasn't desperate and furthermore he wasn't stupid. Even if he liked the idea of seeing her naked, that was the end of it. God save him from any more involvements, physical or otherwise, with ambitious women.

"That's all of it." Her no-nonsense tone snapped him out of his introspection.

"Good thing. If you'd tossed in the kitchen sink I'd have to circle back to pick you up later."

"Or maybe I'd have to read the manual on how to fly your plane."

He laughed at her not-so-subtle message that he was dispensable. "You'd be out of luck there, Doc. My plane doesn't come with a manual."

"How fortuitous then that I left the kitchen sink behind at the last moment."

Dalton was about a hundred percent certain Dr. Skye Shanahan wasn't thrilled to be here. He spent a lot of time hauling strangers from one destination point to another and he'd learned to read body language. Hers screamed that she was here under protest. "I'd say it's a very good thing." He glanced at the mountain of luggage and pushed the cart in the direction of his plane on the tarmac outside. "How long are you staying again?"

She bristled. "I didn't want to leave something I might need."

He skirted a group of guys who had obviously flown in on a hunting trip. They looked like hunters and the rifle cases were a dead giveaway. He'd take that assignment over transporting Dr. Holier Than Thou any day. But he was getting paid and that's what mattered. And while she might be a pain in the ass, she was undisputably easier on the eyes than the hunters.

"I didn't bring this much with me when I moved

here," he said, pretending to stagger under the weight of the bags.

"Then I guess you win the light packer award."

He nodded. "I keep it on my mantel."

"Good place for an award."

"Missed diagnosis, Doc." Her full lips tightened every time he called her Doc. "I keep my suitcase on the mantel." It was actually a lightweight backpack but why let the truth stand in the way of a good story? Tall tales abounded in the Alaskan wilderness.

That seemed to catch her off-guard. "You keep your suitcase on your mantel? How...bohemian."

"Yeah. It keeps me grounded—it reminds me that everything I really need can fit in there."

She looked at him as if he'd belched in public and then cast a faintly mournful eye at the luggage cart. "I hope I've remembered everything I'm going to need."

He held the exit door for her and then damn near lost one of her suitcases wrestling the cart over the threshold. "Doc, I bet when you leave, you won't have used even half of what you brought with you."

She shivered and tugged her wool jacket together over her sweater, whether from chill or apprehension he had no clue. Maybe a combination of both. She tilted her chin up at a stubborn angle. "But I'll have it if I need it."

"Yes, ma'am, that you definitely will." He opened the door of the plane and started stowing her mountain of luggage. "Here we are."

She stepped back and eyed his baby, aghast. "That's a plane?"

There were some lines you didn't cross. You could insult a man's intelligence, his mother, his sister, the size of his private equipment, but you never, ever insulted a bush pilot's plane. "Wings. Propeller. She's not just a plane, she's a damn fine plane." He patted Belinda's riveted metal side.

She narrowed her bewitching eyes at him. "Are you expecting me to *get* on that plane?"

At this point, it'd be easier if he took her luggage and let her hitch-hike her prissy ass to Good Riddance. But that wasn't part of his contract. "That's the general idea."

"But it's so…little."

He was damn proud he managed to not roll his eyes at her. "You were expecting a 747?"

"There weren't any details. I was just told I'd have a connecting flight out of Anchorage." She shrugged and he almost felt sorry for her. She seemed so surprised. It occurred to him that she might be one of those really smart people who was long on brains but got the short end of the common-sense stick.

"You didn't find it strange that the pilot was going to be waiting for you?"

Again, despite her haughtiness, there was a vulnerability about her that surprised him. "Sometimes doctors get preferential treatment. It's not as if I expect it or demand it, but it just happens sometimes. So I really hadn't thought too much about it. I was more concerned with the lack of information available about Good Riddance on the Internet."

He might've been living the simpler life for almost a decade but he still recognized all the trappings of money and privilege. The matching designer luggage. A fine-worsted wool suit. Real gold earrings. Dr. Skye Shanahan had packed and dressed this way for her foray into the Alaskan wilderness? He reconsidered his previous opinion about preferring to take the hunting party in the terminal instead of her. Watching the good doctor get her comeuppance might prove to be fine entertainment for the next few weeks.

He bit back a smirk and offered his hand to help her aboard.

"Haven't you heard, Doc? We're Alaska's best-kept secret."

2

"YOU CAN OPEN YOUR EYES now." Mr. Saunders's voice came through the headset he'd given her to put on before they'd started taxiing down the runway in the tin-can he was passing off as a reputable mode of travel.

She'd worked too damn hard to get through medical school and residency to die now. If they crashed, she just hoped she had time to throttle him with her bare hands before they bit the dust.

But right now, she had a bigger problem. *If* she regurgitated her lunch, and it had been a distinct possibility hurtling down the runway in this rust bucket—which was why she'd squeezed her eyes shut and imagined herself in the E.R. attending a messy gunshot wound, just to ground and stabilize herself—*if* she threw up, she'd have to kill him from abject humiliation alone.

From his smug tone, Mr. Saunders clearly had no idea how close he was skirting death, one way or another. Still, if she went ahead and killed him she'd no longer be plagued by this attraction to him, she thought darkly. That was one way to handle it.

"Relax, Doc. I haven't lost a passenger…yet."

She opened her eyes and blinked at the fast-fading outlay of Anchorage and the splendor of the mountains. "Very amusing, Mr. Saunders. A competent pilot and a comic."

"I throw the comedy in for free." He pointed to the snow-capped slope. "That's Mt. Hood."

She resented him anew. It was just wrong that while barely holding on to her lunch, she was hit with an incredible awareness of Dalton Saunders. It was as if he filled all the space around her with this broad shoulders, his scent, and simply his presence. She didn't like it or her reaction to him worth a damn.

He was just the type of man who'd get her into all types of trouble. She'd come to Good Riddance to do a job, to get her mother off her case, to try to live up to those impossibly high Shanahan expectations that had been shoved down her throat since birth. What wasn't on the agenda was getting into trouble. So the best thing to do was ignore the man in the seat next to her.

"Very nice. I rented a National Geographic video. We're too far west to fly past the Wrangell St. Elias Mountain Range, right?"

He shot her a quick glance and she read a mixture of admiration and surprise in his look. "Right."

"I did as much homework as I could, Mr. Saunders. However, I have next to nothing in the way of information on Good Riddance. Can you fill me in?"

"It was founded by Merrilee Danville Weatherspoon twenty-plus years ago. In that time, the population has exploded to about seven hundred and fifty, give or take a few."

Oh God, it was even worse than she'd imagined. There were more than seven hundred and fifty employees in the medical high-rise that housed her office back home. "I'm afraid to ask, but what kind of amenities are we talking about?"

"Pretty much everything. That's the way it is out here. If we don't have it, then you don't need it. You cut through a lot of crap and clutter that way."

She really disliked people who presumed to know how everyone should live. "One man's clutter may well be another man's necessity." She ran through a quick mental checklist of everything she'd packed. Thank goodness she'd brought it all with her.

He shrugged those impossibly broad shoulders which seemed equally impossibly close in the confines of the winged go-cart he was guiding through the sky. "We have a bar/restaurant right next to Merrilee's place. It makes it easier when the snow's on the ground outside."

"That's it? Two buildings together?" What had she gotten herself into?

"Of course not." His grin held an edge of teasing but also an edge of satisfaction at her dismayed reaction. "There's a hunting and fishing outfitter. And a Laundromat. It's right next to the taxidermy/barber shop/ beauty salon/mortuary."

Instinctively, she touched her hair. She suspected the taxidermist barber didn't charge an arm and a leg, no pun intended, the way some of Atlanta's finest salons did. "The barber shop and beauty salon are part of the taxidermy? And all this is shared with the mortuary?"

"Yeah. You can wind up waiting a week or more for a hair cut during high hunting season."

"Oh. Dear. God." She narrowed her eyes at his profile. There was no mistaking the amused tilt of his well-shaped mouth. Relief flooded her. He was teasing. "Okay. Fine. I get it. A little joke at the expense of the relief doctor."

Another shrug and he nodded to his left. "That's the Sitnusak River. Some of the finest salmon and halibut fishing in the world. Have you ever had fresh halibut, Doc?"

"Not fresh, but of course, I've had halibut."

"You're here just on the tail end of the season, but you'll have to try it at Gus's."

She didn't expect much from anything, fresh or otherwise, prepared at a place in the middle of nowhere by a man named Gus. Nonetheless she aimed for what she hoped wasn't a thoroughly pained smile. "I'm looking forward to it."

"You've got to work on the sincerity, Doc."

She ignored his comment. "So, Mr. Saunders, how long have you lived in Good Riddance?"

"I'm working on nine years, Doc. It was the best move I ever made."

She was seriously flummoxed. Of all the places in

the world, why would someone choose to move to the middle of nowhere? It was like taking a giant step backward. "But how'd you wind up in Good Riddance?"

"I liked the town philosophy so I stayed."

Technically, he hadn't answered her question, but she wasn't going to push it.

"And that philosophy is…?"

"Good Riddance is where you leave behind whatever troubles you."

She spoke without thinking. "It sounds like a cult."

His laughter in the headset startled her, nearly sending her jumping out of her skin. "No cult here. Just the offer of a fresh start."

Fresh start. That had an ominous ring. Who went somewhere so remote for a fresh start except for people who didn't want to be found? Or those wanting to adopt a hermit lifestyle. But Mr. Saunders didn't strike her as hermit-like. While her parents were both insanely practical, pragmatic individuals, Skye had inherited her grandmother Shanahan's active imagination and it was now in overdrive.

"Fresh start?" she echoed.

"Yeah, you know sometimes you just want to put the past and the mistakes you made behind you. Haven't you ever felt the urge to reinvent yourself, Dr. Shanahan? To go to a place where no one knows you, a place where you can become whomever and whatever you want to be, without any expectations?"

For a few illicit seconds she indulged in the notion of simply being. She'd always been Skye Shanahan, daughter of the brilliant and esteemed Drs. Edward and Margaret Shanahan and sister of the equally brilliant Patrick Shanahan. Expectation had been her intimate acquaintance since birth. She felt as if Dalton Saunders had peered into her very soul, had connected with her in a way no one had before. And that simply wouldn't do. She did not want to connect with him, didn't want to feel this emotional intimacy. She rejected the notion they could share similar experiences and came up with her own interpretation of his past, one far, far removed from hers.

"Were you in prison?"

He paused for a moment as if deciding just how much to answer and she wasn't sure she'd get an answer at all. She'd read that Alaska appealed to a whole different kind of person. And there was something of an outlaw element, at least that was her impression from articles she'd read on-line. She found herself holding her breath for his response.

"Yep. I definitely served my time and Good Riddance was exactly what I needed when I got out." He shook his head, as if trying to forget. "If we were flying farther north, you'd see an ancient caribou migration route. That's what you see in Alaska."

"Interesting." She was more interested, however, in what he'd done time for but the obvious subject change told her he'd said all he was going to. A shiver ran down her spine. Still, she reassured herself his crime couldn't have been too bad. He was fairly young, she'd estimate early to mid-thirties based on the crinkle lines at the corners of his eyes. If he'd done something truly heinous, he'd still be sitting in the slammer. Wouldn't he?

The plane suddenly lurched and she thought her stomach contents might find their way into her lap. "Are we going down?" she yelled, clutching the strap to her right. "I need a parachute."

"Easy, Doc. We're fine. That was just a little patch of turbulence. I'm sure you've hit stuff like this flying in the big boys before but it feels a whole lot more personal in a smaller plane."

His smug amusement scraped along her nerve endings. She was far from proud of the way she'd behaved, yelling in panic, but her training didn't encompass crashing in a Cracker Jack toy plane in the middle of Remoteville, her only companion a man who'd done hard time. And that was only if they didn't die.

"How much longer until we're there?" It felt as if they'd been flying forever.

"Maybe a quarter of an hour."

"Oh."

"There's a problem?"

"Well, I don't see anything around yet."

"Nope."

Her head was beginning to throb. Maybe it was an altitude thing. She scrambled in her bag, found the travel ibuprofen and swallowed two without benefit of a drink.

"Headache?" he asked.

She glanced across the space separating them. He boasted an attractive profile—rugged jaw and a nice nose with a faint hump in the middle that led her to believe it'd been broken at some point in time. The errant thought danced through her head that he'd produce lovely children. Dear God, where had that thought come from? His potential offspring had absolutely nothing to do with her. "Yes," she said, confirming her headache, then deliberately looking away from his too-handsome profile.

Outside her window, wilderness sprawled before her. Some people might find this enthralling, exciting, but she preferred her back-to-nature experiences to be those of sitting in her cozy den watching National Geographic specials. *This* was not her cup of tea—Starbucks, venti, black, sweet Tazo with light ice—*that* was her cup of tea.

The plane suddenly banked sharply to her right. Saunders's voice was in her ear. "Look to your right and you'll see something very few people are privileged to see in person. That's a grizzly salmon fishing."

Unfortunately, her stomach banked right along with the plane. She could clamp a spewing artery. She could reattach a missing digit. She could clean a gangrenous wound, but this, she couldn't handle this. She caught a glimpse of a huge, brown thing but all she could think was, quite inanely, that if Saunders looked to *his* right, he was about to see something very few people were privileged to see in person, as well.

Without further ado, Dr. Skye Shanahan promptly tossed her cookies. Or to be pathologically correct, her lunch of tuna on whole wheat.

HE'D SEEN WORSE. Much worse. He'd seen grown, macho men lose it in a small plane. He'd seen Elmer Driscoll get knee-crawling drunk and lose it behind Gus's place last week. But he'd never seen anyone more frustrated with having lost it.

"You okay?" he asked as she stepped out of the copse of trees wearing a pair of black slacks and a coppery brown sweater that seemed to pick up the highlights in her red hair, her toothbrush and mouthwash clutched in one hand, her soiled suit and sweater in the other.

He'd radioed in an emergency landing and promptly set the plane down. There was no way in hell he was showing up at Good Riddance with a puke-covered passenger. His reputation as a pilot would suffer, and her reputation as a physician who should be made of stronger stuff, would suffer even worse. And she'd never forgive him for the humiliation, which was neither here nor there, except who knew if he might turn up sick or injured in the ensuing weeks and her Hippocratic oath might take a back seat to the memory of arriving in town covered in barf.

While she'd changed clothes and cleaned up behind the cover of fir trees and a small stream adjacent to the meadow he'd landed in, he'd taken care of the plane.

"Do you think you could manage not to roll the plane anymore? Have you ever heard of a straight and level course, Saunders?"

He silently thanked the powers that be for her haughtiness. It simply reinforced for him that, no matter how damn attractive he found her, she wasn't the woman for him. "You could've told me you were feeling sick. Better yet, have you ever heard of Dramamine, Shanahan?"

"I wasn't aware I had a problem with motion sickness...until now."

A piece of the fir tree sticking out of her hair offset her haughty embarrassment. By rights, he should've let her greet the inhabitants of Good Riddance sprouting an evergreen. However, he simply couldn't. He reached over to pluck it from her hair. "Hold on a moment."

It turned out the piece of tree wasn't caught up in her hair but in the clip. Her hair tumbled down in a red cascade, settling below her shoulders. She gasped and he simply stood there, transfixed, at a loss for words.

All thoughts of haughtiness and wrong choices flew out of his head. She was, quite simply, stunning, standing in a meadow ringed by trees, with the glinting sun picking out radiant strands of gold in her red hair, her eyes taking on the hue and depth of magnificent glacier ice that had spent millenniums forming.

For one millisecond or it could've been a lifetime, Dalton was lost. Lost in those eyes and that hair and... well, lost in her. For one crazy moment in time he wanted to bridge the short physical distance separating them. He wanted to kiss her gorgeous mouth, bury his hands in the living fire of her hair, peel away the layers of her clothes and connect all her freckles with a trail of kisses. Then he wanted to make slow, sweet love to this prickly pear of a woman who, although she was standing less than a foot from him, was nonetheless worlds apart from him. He wanted to lay her down in the grass of an untainted meadow, with only the sun and sky and the occasional soaring bird of prey as witness to their union.

In short, he wanted Dr. Skye Shanahan like he'd never wanted anything.

Her eyes widened and for a moment he thought he saw an answering need. And then she slammed the proverbial door.

"What are you doing, Saunders?"

He realized he was holding on to the twig, which still had her clip attached. He held it up the way hunters displayed trophy kills. "This was in your hair. I didn't think you wanted to show up with an evergreen branch sticking out of your head."

"No, I didn't. But it would've been nice if you hadn't destroyed my hairdo in the meantime."

Yet again, he wanted to kiss her, but this time for yanking him back to reality with her shrewish tongue. "Do you hear that, Shanahan?"

She narrowed her eyes and cocked her head to one side, a flash of panic shadowing her features. "What? I don't hear anything. Is it a bear?"

"No. I thought I heard a faint and distant thank-you, one without any recriminations behind it. I guess it was just wishful thinking on my part."

"Have you considered that had you not been hot-dogging, I wouldn't have gotten sick? And if I hadn't gotten sick, I wouldn't have needed to hike into the wilderness and clean up in an ice-cold river? And I wouldn't have had to worry about getting branches in my hair?"

This was rich. "So, the fact that a doctor can't diagnose and properly treat her own motion sickness or at least acknowledge it and give her pilot a heads up is *my* fault?"

"You could use some sensitivity training, Saunders. And I've never, ever had an issue with motion sickness before."

So far, in the course of less than an hour, she'd managed to paint him a felon, an incompetent pilot and insult the hell out of his plane. He'd had enough. "Any chance you're knocked up, Doc? Wait. No man could get past that barbed tongue of yours to get the job done." He foolishly, dangerously thought that under different circumstances he'd be at the front of the line to give it a try. But then again, Dalton had never been able to resist a challenge.

A blush definitely stained her face. "Saunders, do you think you could pretend to be a professional and get me to Good Riddance without further mishap?"

"Doc, it's my raison d'être. By the way, I learned that phrase in prison." She'd been so quick to decide he must have a checkered past. He wasn't too damned sure Dr. Stick Up Her Ass would understand the concept of a metaphorical prison, so he'd let her roll with what she wanted to think. He'd been imprisoned in the corporate culture, the rat race, but he didn't think she'd get that. Although he'd bet Belinda, his trusty plane, that Shanahan was doing the same time he'd been doing.

She strode toward the plane, her back ramrod straight. But her hair and eyes had told him a different story. She had passion.

"Just get me there, Saunders. I thought I'd never hear myself say it, but I'm ready to be in Good Riddance."

3

"YOU MUST BE THE NEW relief doc," said a sixtyish woman with blond hair who stepped forward to greet Skye. Every eye in the room had trained on Skye the moment she'd walked through the door of Good Riddance Air Field/Restaurant/Bed and Breakfast. "I'm Merrilee Danville Weatherspoon, founder and mayor."

Ms. Weatherspoon had a melodic, distinctly Southern voice which somehow fit with the fact that the woman's flannel shirt had lace trim around the collar and down the front and lace-trimmed flannel curtains hung at the windows of the log building. Skye liked her immediately.

"Dr. Skye Shanahan. Nice to meet you."

"On behalf of the town, I'd like to welcome you to Good Riddance, Alaska, where you get to leave behind whatever troubles you."

Two older men sporting caps and beards sat in rocking chairs across the room next to a pot-bellied stove, a chess table between them. On the multicolored, braided rug at their feet, a couple of thickly furred huskies lay curled in tight balls. Both dogs looked at her and then closed their eyes again. In one corner, a TV played a soap opera that no one was watching.

A very attractive man, obviously of native heritage given his skin-tone, short dark hair and flat-broad cheek-bones, sat propped on the edge of the desk that held neat stacks of paperwork and two-way radio equipment, a schedule clasped in his hands. He stepped forward and offered a brief handshake. "Clint Sisnuket. Pleased to meet you."

She returned the greeting. Disconcertingly, his touch didn't send a little shiver down her spine the way Saunders's had…did…whatever.

Everyone offered up a hello. But it was the *where you get to leave behind whatever troubles you* that stuck with Skye. That was rich in irony as what troubled Skye specifically was being in Good Riddance in the first place. However, even she possessed enough common sense and social skills, although she'd sometimes been accused of lacking both, not to say so. "I'm pleased to be here."

See, she could tell a white lie as well as the next person. And it wasn't too much of a stretch to admit that she was glad to be back on terra firma—and doubly glad to be out of Dalton Saunders's company.

Speaking of the devil…Saunders strolled in at that moment. "Afternoon, Merrilee. Where do you want the Doc's bags? She's got one or two."

He could save his sarcasm for someone else. She

wasn't amused. Well, perhaps she might be amused if he was someone else. But *he* got her back up.

"Just put them in the back of your pickup, Dalton. We've had a little complication, resulting in a change of plan."

"Complication?" Saunders said.

"Change of plan?" Skye had a bad feeling.

"The roof caved in on the guest rooms upstairs." Merrilee shook her head. "It's just as well Scat Murphy left town when he did or I'd have kicked him out anyway for substandard work." One could only surmise that Scat—and why would anyone trust someone whose name, given or otherwise, was equated with excrement—had done some roofing or sheetrocking. "Bull—" another name right up there with Scat, she thought "—is doing a patch job now but it's going to take nearly a week to get it done right." The mayor patted Skye on the shoulder. "Don't you worry, though. We're going to put you up in Irene Marbut's cabin out at Shadow Lake."

At least she had a nice normal name. "Ms. Marbut won't mind a stranger barging in?"

"Well, dear, Irene died a few months ago so I think she'll be fine with it. Gus went out a few hours ago with Luellen Sisnuket, Clint's cousin," she said, nodding to the dark-haired man at the desk's edge, "and got the place ready for you. Well, as ready as they could in such a short time. It was the darnedest thing. I was about to go upstairs this morning to put fresh linens on your bed." She leaned forward in a confiding manner. "Bull says it's procrastination but I always wait until the morning of a new arrival to change the sheets so they're as fresh as possible." She straightened. "Anyhow, I was on my way upstairs when I heard a huge bang. If I'd been two minutes earlier, I'd have been in a world of hurt."

"Then I'm glad you waited." She didn't know what else to say. Now she was staying in a dead woman's cabin "out on" a lake. Skye didn't miss that nuance. Good Riddance was already off the beaten path in every sense of the word. She couldn't imagine what would qualify as "out" for these people. And though she was familiar with the dead, she didn't, as a matter of course, sleep in their beds. It was a little creepy.

Merrilee offered another shoulder pat. "Yes, ma'am. All's well that ends well. We've got you fixed right up, honey. Dalton here can give you a ride in to work every morning and drop you off in the evenings, seeing as how you're going to be his neighbor. He took good care of Ms. Irene until she passed and he'll take good care of you while you're here. Isn't that right, Dalton?"

"Dalton?" she echoed, her voice sounding weak even to her own ears. "Neighbor?" This situation was going from bad to worse. "What about other people in the area?" she asked, a sick feeling, dread rather than nausea, gathering in the pit of her empty stomach.

"There's nobody else, dear. You'll have all the privacy you want. Out at Shadow Lake, you can get away from the hustle and bustle of Good Riddance."

How much *hustle and bustle* could there be in a town that didn't appear to even have a traffic light? She stifled rising hysteria. It was bad enough to be sent to this God-forsaken town, but now she was about to be stuck in a dead woman's cabin on the edge of some lake, solely dependent on an ex-convict. Somebody just take a gun and shoot her. Wait, in this area, someone might be all too willing. "It sounds lovely," she said, her voice faint.

"You can really indulge your inner pioneer spirit," Merrilee said with a wide smile.

"My inner pioneer spirit?" Skye repeated and mustered a weak smile. She didn't possess a single ounce of pioneer spirit. Nope. None. "Um…there is running water, isn't there?"

"No worries, Doc," Saunders said with what might appear to be a friendly smile to the rest of the room but which she *knew* to be an evil smirk. "It's not that far to carry the bucket to the lake. And I'll show you how to rub the flint together to start a fire. Just think of all that Girl Scout training you can put to use."

"A bucket to the lake? Flint?" She surreptitiously pinched herself just to make sure she hadn't fallen into a nightmare even worse than the recurring one she often had, where she showed up at a medical conference naked.

"Hush, Dalton." Merrilee waved a hand at the bush pilot. "You're scaring her to death. Don't pay him any attention, honey. He's just joshing you. Irene put in running water at the same time Dalton did. And the electricity might be iffy sometimes, but we all use matches instead of flint. I'll send you out with a pack just in case."

Skye said nothing because she wasn't so sure she could muster anything outside of a wail.

But it didn't really matter because Ms. Merrilee Danville Weatherspoon filled what was almost a conversational gap.

"Are you hungry, honey?"

As if on cue, Skye's empty stomach growled. "I could eat."

"Dalton, I'm taking Dr. Skye—you don't mind if I call you that, do you, honey? With those lovely eyes you look like a Dr. Skye instead of a stuffy Dr. Shanahan—" How could she tell this transplanted steel magnolia no? "—over to Gus's for a bite of dinner before y'all head out. That was the plan before the roof caved in upstairs anyway. Can you give us about an hour?"

"No problem, Merrilee. It'll take at least that long to move all of her luggage from the plane to the truck."

Merrilee swatted at Saunders. Too bad she missed—someone needed to smack the smug look right off his ruggedly handsome face. Did everyone in Good Riddance know about his record? Probably no one cared. That's what these outposts of civilization were like, populated by misfits and miscreants.

She realized suddenly that she was starving, having lost her lunch earlier. Dinner at Gus's would probably prove to be worse than a fast-food drive-thru but it would be food. And food would be good right now.

She could only pray that Saunders drove a truck better than he piloted a plane. And she absolutely refused to think about the fact that she was going to spend the next week living close to a man she found altogether too attractive for her own good.

DALTON HEAVED THE LAST of the suitcases into the bed of the pickup truck and headed toward Gus's. Bull Swenson fell into step beside him. "You brought the new Doc in today, eh? She's a looker. I saw her from upstairs."

Dalton was altogether too aware of just what a looker the new doc was.

"She's an acid-tongued shrew." He knew whatever he said to Bull would stay with Bull, except for bits and pieces that might trickle through to Merrilee. Merrilee had a way of pulling information out of people and since she and Bull had been an item longer than Dalton had been around, chances were Merrilee would soon know how he felt about the good doctor. But Dalton didn't care.

Shanahan was what she was—an acid-tongued shrew in a tempting package of red hair, blue eyes and a nicely rounded figure. However, he knew only a crazy man would wade into the frigid waters of Shanahan Bay, although he'd been sorely tempted to do just that earlier today. There'd be something seriously wrong with a man who actually sought out her company.

Bull rumbled, which was his version of a chuckle. "She reminds me of Merrilee when I first met her, fresh out of the lower forty-eight and full of piss and vinegar."

"Merrilee full of piss and vinegar?" Merrilee was strong. Any woman who elected to live in the Alaskan bush had to be made of stern stuff. "She's determined and she's got an iron backbone but…"

"Yep. I'd say that sums up Dr. Skye."

Dalton preferred to think of her as Shanahan but then again he could only imagine that the Dr. Skye tag would annoy her almost as much as being called Doc. Still, Dalton hadn't been referring to her.

"No. I meant Merrilee has an iron backbone."

"That she does. But Dr. Skye does, too."

"How would you know that about the Doc already?"

Bull slanted him a look from beneath his bushy grey eyebrows. "At my age, there aren't many things that can surprise me when it comes to people."

The Doc wasn't as tough as Bull thought. Alaska was going to chew Skye Shanahan up and spit her out. "She tossed it on the trip in. I had to land at Bear Claw point to let her clean up."

Bull laughed, but it wasn't an unkind laugh at Doc's expense. Actually, Dalton got the distinct impression the joke was on him. Bull clapped a meaty hand across Dalton's back. After eight years Dalton was prepared— the first time it had sent him flying. "Son, a backbone of steel doesn't necessarily extend to the belly. Did I ever tell you about the time I signed on for a fishing season with Cap'n Louis Montrique?"

Dalton shook his head. Bull got a faraway look in his eye. "It was in '72 and I'd come up from Laredo, Texas. Alaska was something then. A man could find breathing room. I'd heard you could make good money in a short period of time working one of the fishing boats. I lost thirty pounds—puked every pound off. I've never been so sick in my life, but I'd been hired to do a job so I learned fast to haul in a net while feeding the fishes. They don't hire extra hands so there's no one to pick up any slack. Every man's got to carry his own load. But my point is, I'm as tough as they come, but motion sickness, it doesn't take any prisoners. Don't go judging Doc Skye too harshly."

Bull was one of the toughest men Dalton knew. It wasn't something Bull discussed, but it was common knowledge to everyone in Good Riddance that the man had spent two years at the Hanoi Hilton, courtesy of the Vietcong, back during the Vietnam War. It didn't take much to figure those memories were one of things Bull wanted to bid Good Riddance to when he settled here. The Doc had obviously won Bull over at "hello" which was saying something. Bull was known for being an excellent judge of character.

"Okay," Dalton said. "We'll see."

They climbed the two wooden stairs lit by a blinking neon sign declaring the locale to be Augustina's—commonly known near and far as Gus's.

Gus hailed them the moment they walked in the door. "Evening, gentlemen. They're waiting for you over there in the corner," she said, nodding toward the right. "The crowd just died down. Y'all want the regular?"

"Sure thing," Dalton said.

Bull nodded. "Much obliged."

They crossed the scarred wooden floor to the booth

where Merrilee and the Doc sat across from one another. The rest of Gus's looked the way it usually did,
crowded but with everyone doing their own thing. Two
pool tables in the back had games going on. In the far
corner, Brody and Tyrrell Initkit had challenged one another to a dart game. Food and drinks were being served
and Frank Sinatra was crooning a tune over the radio.
That's what happened when everyone knew everyone
else. Even though the radio station was two hundred
fifty miles west of Good Riddance, Gus had requested
"dinner music" from six until nine every evening and
so dinner music they had.

Bull slid into the booth next to Merrilee, leaving Dalton to fill the slot next to the Doc. His knee brushed hers
and instant heat tracked through him. Next time he'd
be sure to sit across from her. Keeping some distance
between himself and Skye Shanahan struck him as a
good idea. He drew a deep breath and found himself
inhaling her scent. Make that a damn good idea.

FINALLY THE CROWD OF people that had surrounded
them—God, she'd never remember all of the names, it
was worse than a medical conference—had dispersed
when Dalton and a man who could have doubled for
Grizzly Adams waltzed in.

Welcome to the land where nothing was as it seemed.
Instead of the grizzled old man Skye had been expecting, Gus had turned out to be a woman in her mid-to-late
twenties, whose dark hair was threaded dramatically
with a shock of white in the front.

The establishment itself was crowded but immaculately clean. Booths hugged the "front" and right walls. Tables with chairs filled the center. A long bar, complete with a highly polished brass foot rail, provided a focal point. To the left of the open kitchen, a small stage stood between two pool tables and a dart board area. The entry from Merrilee's was over by the stage. Merrilee had explained that Thursday karaoke was big around here. Skye shuddered at the very thought.

Her head was spinning and she could've gotten by quite nicely without Saunders's aggravating, albeit disturbingly attractive, presence next to her in the booth. However, there was nothing she could do about it, short of being rude. And if he was going to be her nearest neighbor, that didn't seem the smartest plan.

Merrilee introduced the latest mountain man. "Dr. Skye, this is Bull Swenson. Bull, Dr. Skye. She's filling in for Dr. Morrow while he's on vacation."

She offered her hand across the table. "Pleased to meet you…" She hesitated, finding it difficult to actually refer to him as Bull, "Mr. Swenson."

While his hand swallowed hers, it was a gentle touch. "Pleased to have you here, Doc. And please, call me Bull."

"Bull," she murmured.

Gus arrived with two draft beers which she promptly served to Saunders and Bull.

"Tonight's on the house, Dr. Skye. We've got caribou scaloppini or a moose ragout. Or I can whip you up an omelet if you'd prefer."

"The scaloppini is to die for," Bull said, seemingly serious.

Wild game scaloppini and ragout? Maybe these were some kind of Alaskan frozen dinners. "Scaloppini would be lovely," she said.

"You know I love your scaloppini. That's what I want," Saunders said, slanting a charming smile Gus's way. That smile qualified as disarming, dangerous... even downright lethal. For a second she wondered if there might be something between the bush pilot and the bar owner. But no, there didn't seem to be any particular sparks flying there. And it was sheer stupidity that a feeling of relief chased close on that realization.

"I think I've got a taste for moose tonight, so I'll take the ragout," Bull said, picking up his beer and taking a swallow.

"Merrilee?"

"Would you mind terribly if I order that mushroom omelet with brie and gorgonzola?"

"Of course not. Chanterelles or shitake mushrooms?"

"Both?"

Gus shook her head. "It's a bastardization, but because it's you, I'll do it."

Gus bustled off and Skye looked to Merrilee for clarification.

"Gus is my niece." Skye would never have guessed. She wasn't seeing the family resemblance, but then sometimes that's just the way it was.

"Gus trained in Paris," Bull added.

Surely he didn't mean *trained?* "Trained?"

"You know, got her degree from the L'Ecole Gastronomique," Saunders explained, as if she were simpleminded. Skye appreciated good food but she'd never heard of the L'Ecole Gastronomique. Still, she'd rather lose a limb than confess that to the smug Saunders, so she nodded as if she was intimately acquainted with the cooking school.

"She trained in Paris and then came to Good Riddance?" Skye asked. This place was full of some truly odd people.

Merrilee and Bull exchanged a subtle glance which Skye almost missed. "She worked in Manhattan for a while before she came here."

"She was working in Manhattan when Miriam sent her here."

Bull chuckled, at least that's what she thought it was, and shook his head. "She fell in love with the town her Aunt Merrilee had founded and decided to stay."

Skye sipped at her wine. She wasn't big on alcohol, but right now she really needed a drink. "How did that happen? I mean, it's not every day that a woman wanders into the middle of nowhere and founds a town." Or maybe it was out here.

"I'd been married for twelve years when I finally figured out it was a whopper of a mistake. Since I couldn't kill him—well, I could've but I didn't want to wind up in the slammer—I decided to pack my belongings and move as far away as I could and still retain my U.S. citizenship. Everybody thought I'd lost my mind. So I took our R.V. and started driving. I knew I'd know when I found where I belonged.

"One thing led to another. I took a wrong turn off the highway and stopped to spend the night here and I just knew. I knew I'd found the place for me. Word gets out in these parts when a single woman arrives and before long, other people started showing up. So there you have it. My ex told everyone I had a mid-life crisis but I was just finding where I belonged and it wasn't with him."

Skye nodded, but she was sure she hadn't heard the whole story. It was just a gut instinct but a strong one, nonetheless. Gus arrived bearing plates as artfully arranged as any Skye had seen in the best restaurants. It smelled heavenly. After one bite, she knew it tasted even better than it smelled.

A rough-hewn timber building, a clientele wearing blue-jeans and work boots and a five-star quality meal.

Welcome to Good Riddance, Alaska.

4

SAUNDERS FOLDED HIS NAPKIN and placed it on the table next to his plate. "We'd better be heading out," he said. "I've got an early flight in the morning which means Doc—" she wanted to throttle him every time he called her that "—has to be up early too. What time does Nelson get in?"

Merrilee dabbed at her mouth with the edge of her white linen cloth. "What time does he need to be there?"

"Six-thirty."

"I'll give him a call," Merrilee said with a brief nod.

Even though this was about her, Skye was fairly clueless. And she didn't do clueless. "Nelson?"

"Your assistant, dear." Merrilee reached across the table and patted her hand.

"Ah. I see." Actually, she didn't see anything. It was as if she'd stepped through the rabbit hole. Nothing was as it seemed. She'd just had one of the finest meals she'd ever indulged in and now it was time to find out what else was in store for her.

She'd been dreading going to the cabin that was to be her home for the next two weeks. But heck, considering the meal she'd just enjoyed, it might turn out to be a first-rate accommodation—fluffy down pillows, five-hundred-thread-count sheets, a down mattress topper so thick you sank into the bed and never wanted to crawl out….

"Are you okay?" Saunders interrupted her reverie.

"What?"

"It sounded like you moaned." Was that a strained look on his face?

"I most certainly did not."

He slid out of the booth and stood. "Let's go. It'll take half the night to get your suitcases in."

Skye was ready. She'd been desperately aware of Saunders's heat, the breadth of his shoulders and the proximity of his body throughout dinner. She grabbed her jacket and scooted across the wood seat while Bull and Merrilee watched in amusement. "I'd like to thank Gus, if you don't mind."

He shrugged into his jacket. "Make it quick, Shanahan."

Wow, she'd like to smack him. Which was a much better idea than kissing him… Unfortunately, that crazy thought had gone through her head a couple of times over dinner. Instead, she said good-night to the other couple, then stopped by the kitchen, which was open to the rest of the room except for the separating counter. Gus stood at the stove stirring a sauce in a small pan.

"Thank you. That was wonderful."

"You're welcome. I saw you looking at Merrilee's omelet. Want me to send one over to the office tomorrow morning for breakfast? I doubt you'll have time to whip up much for yourself."

Time or not, Skye wasn't much for whipping anything up—she was something of a dud in the kitchen. She ate mainly take-out at home, she'd never had anything that compared to the meal she'd had tonight. "That would be wonderful."

"I'd suggest chanterelles."

Ah, the chanterelle versus shitake situation. Skye didn't volunteer that she wasn't a mushroom purist and wouldn't know the difference. Instead she simply beamed at Gus and said, "Chanterelles would be lovely."

"Sourdough or challah toast? I'm not making the cinnamon rolls until day after tomorrow. I'll put one of those aside for you. There's always a run on them."

Oh. My. God. She might stay for the food alone. Perish that wild, errant thought. No food was that good. However, she was partial to the egg-based bread. "Challah, please."

"Nelson makes a decent cup of coffee so you'll be fine on that front." Without missing a beat, Gus poured the sauce over the contents of the plate.

"Thank you."

"Nice to have you here, Dr. Skye."

"Er, um, nice to be here, Gus." She realized she had no clue what Gus's last name was. Not that she supposed it really mattered. Convention and ceremony seemed out of place here.

Saunders was waiting by the door, engaged in conversation with Merrilee. Her heart sort of did a trippy kind of thing, which once again, made no sense. He was no taller than any other man in the establishment. In fact there were quite a few who were taller and brawnier. He was dressed the same as most of the other men—blue jeans, flannel shirt and boots. But something made him stand out, stand apart, and sent her heart into arrhythmia. Or maybe she was just suffering a mild case of indigestion. She immediately mentally apologized to Gus.

"Ready, Doc?"

"Lead the way."

Saunders shot her a look. What? Did he think she totally lacked any sense of humor?

It was dark when they stepped outside. Really, really dark. "There aren't any streetlights," she said.

He shrugged. "The town voted on it, but the consensus was that we didn't want any light pollution messing with the beauty of the night sky."

Half a dozen streetlights, which would probably cover the town from pillar to post, constituted light pollution? Oh, boy. At this point, she considered herself lucky they didn't find electricity too intrusive.

Biting her tongue, Skye kept pace with Saunders as he led the way back to his waiting pickup, which looked about the same age as her grandmother. She suspected her grandmother was in better shape. Actually, his vehicle was pretty much the same as the rest of the trucks parked along the street. The passenger door creaked and groaned—it sounded like her grandmother, too—when he opened it for her in a shocking display of good manners. Okay, so he wasn't a *total* cretin.

"Thank you," she murmured as he closed her door.

Crossing around the front of the truck, he climbed into the driver's seat and cranked the vehicle. "Got to let her warm up for a minute or two," he said.

Skye nodded, her day starting to catch up with her. She was past ready to get where they were going.

"You'll be able to see better tomorrow but your office is down that way. It's right across from Donna's Repair Center. We try to keep all the repairs in one area of town."

"Very funny." Actually it was fairly funny. Unfortunately, it upped his attraction factor, which was so not what she needed.

A tall gorgeous blond woman made her way up the sidewalk. "In fact, there's Donna now."

Donna and Saunders exchanged waves. Skye suddenly felt terribly dowdy. "Wow, she's stunning. She could do runway work." What was the woman doing running a repair shop? She must be at least 6'3". And that was in flats. Skye had noticed.

Donna disappeared through Gus's front door.

Saunders put the truck in gear and pulled out into the street. "Donna's happy doing what she's doing. Up until five years ago, Donna was Don. Don was the star quarterback at his university but he was very unhappy."

Oh. "Cross dresser?"

"Nope. Full change of equipment."

"Wow." Oddly enough, she'd never actually met a transgender case until she arrived in this small town. "And everyone's okay with that? I'd have thought a big city would be more…accepting."

"That's because you don't know the people of Good Riddance yet," Saunders said.

Moonlight and headlights revealed a curve in the narrow road that was flanked by trees now that they'd left the town behind. It also revealed his strong, masculine profile. "So how far is it to Shadow Lake?" Skye asked. They couldn't get there soon enough. She was achingly aware of every breath he drew.

"Right around ten miles."

It was going to be a long ten miles. She just needed to focus on something, anything, rather than the curve of his fingers around the steering wheel and his occasional flash of a smile. "And you're my closest neighbor?"

"I'm your only neighbor."

The thought set off butterflies in her stomach. "So I guess it's a safe bet there's no light pollution."

"None."

Skye was rather desperate to fill the space between them with conversation, as if that could keep the attraction she felt for him at bay. "What happened to the woman who lived in the cabin?"

"She died in her sleep with a smile on her face."

"There was a smile on her face? How old was she?"

"She was eighty-eight. Why?"

Skye was a woman of science. She told herself she didn't believe in ghosts but she couldn't discount the fact that she was Irish through and through, and a good deal of her grandmother's superstition had found fertile ground in Skye's mind when she was growing up. So, she was darn glad to hear that Ms. Irene probably hadn't departed this earth with any unfinished business that might necessitate her sticking around the cabin. "Just curious. How'd you come to live next door?"

Saunders hit a pothole and her shoulder bounced against the door.

"Sorry about that. You okay?"

She rubbed her shoulder. She'd probably have a bruise but in the big scheme of things… "I'm fine."

"Ms. Irene and her twin sister Erlene moved to Alaska after they both retired from the postal service in Idaho Falls. They couldn't live with one another, but they couldn't stand to be too far apart, so they built cabins out on Shadow Lake. They raised some of the finest sled dogs in Alaska for years. Erlene was the oldest woman to ever complete the Iditarod. She died about six years ago. I'd been looking at a float plane and needed somewhere to keep one, so I rented her cabin and moved in with the understanding I'd dock my plane on Shadow Lake. And I kept an eye on Ms. Irene."

"Away from the hustle and bustle of Good Riddance. So you have a float plane, as well?"

"Nope. Decided not to buy it when I found out there were loons on the lake."

Obviously she'd missed something. "What did the loons have to do with you buying a float plane?"

"Do you know anything about loons?"

"Only that they're birds. They sort of look like ducks, don't they?"

She caught his nod in the moonlight. "Loons are interesting birds. They mate for life and return to the same site to breed every year. A float plane could've interfered with that."

"You didn't buy a plane because of a pair of loons?"

"Hey, they were here first."

"It wasn't a criticism, Saunders. I was just clarifying. I find it admirable. I'm assuming loons are where the term crazy as a loon comes from?"

"Not exactly. You ever heard a loon?"

"Not that I know of."

"Oh, you'd know. It's a very distinct sound. You'll hear them. We've had unseasonably warm weather and they'll head south soon, but they should be here for another few days. I hope."

Without warning, he braked to a stop in the middle of the road.

"What are you doing?"

He nodded toward the windshield. "Moose."

It was huge and ugly and standing in their path, nonchalantly eating what looked like a small tree growing beside the road. She'd never been a Rocky and Bull-winkle fan. "Okay. Can you make it go away?"

"Nope."

It had been a long day. Traveling always wore her out. She really needed a good night's sleep and some distance away from Dalton Saunders—she was sure both would go a long way in reining in her awareness of this man. She was simply tired now which left her defenses compromised. "What do you mean you can't?"

"It's rutting season."

"What? Will he confuse you for a female?"

"Shanahan, did you skip the course on sexual behavior in med school?"

"It was med school, Saunders, not vet school."

"Rutting season means he's ready to fight. And in a fight with a bull moose, I'd come out on the losing end."

"So what do we do?"

He killed the engine. "We wait."

RUTTING SEASON. MAYBE that was his problem. Man co-existed much more closely with nature in Alaska. Perhaps some of the mating season fever had caught because he was almost painfully aware of Skye Shanahan sitting next to him. And now they were alone, in the moonlight, waiting for the moose to finish foraging.

"How long before he's going to be through?"

Not soon enough. He was thoroughly disgusted with himself. He was damn near fascinated by her and that was just stupid—she was precisely the kind of woman he'd left behind when he'd checked out of the lower forty-eight. And there was no room in his life for stupid. His frustration with himself and the situation—he damn sure hadn't counted on having her living in the cabin next to him—gave way to sarcasm. "Here, I'll consult my crystal ball and let you know."

"Surliness is totally unnecessary."

She was right, which made it all the worse. "This is not some zoo creature we trotted out for you, Shanahan. He's a wild animal. He'll be through when he's not hungry anymore. I have no idea how long it's going to take until he satisfies that appetite and decides to take care of the other."

Dammit to hell if that didn't conjure up images of clothes being taken off and windows fogging up, of rolling around on his bench seat naked and sweaty with Shanahan.

"Well…I…uh…hope he finishes soon. It's been a long day and I'm ready for a hot shower. After traveling all day, I feel like a germ magnet."

His newfound imagination readily came up with that image, as well. He gritted his teeth. "Yep, nothing like a hot shower at the end of a long, hard day."

The moon, riding high in the October sky brought her hair to life. "It's gone."

"What's gone?" he asked, bemused by her hair, her mouth, her very closeness.

"The moose. He's gone."

"Oh, yeah, he is." He started the truck and threw it in gear.

"So, it seems like everyone in Good Riddance is running from something," she said.

Talk about switching conversational tracks. But he supposed between himself, Donna and Merrilee, he could see where she might get that impression.

"Everyone, everywhere is either running from something or to something. The trick is figuring out what that something is."

His story was pretty common knowledge around town, but he'd never divulged the part about finding Lauren in bed with his boss. That stayed with him. He suspected there was more to Merrilee's story than everyone knew, as well. He wondered what Skye Shanahan was running from. Dalton was fairly certain not even she had a clue. Maybe she'd figure it out while she was here. Alaska seemed to have that effect on people.

He made a right-hand turn at the towering spruce that marked the driveway to Shadow Lake.

"Here we are. Home sweet home."

5

SKYE STARED AT THE CARIBOU that eyed her from where it was mounted over the fireplace. Numerous other dead animals lined the cabin walls. A stuffed fox stood next to the hearth. She didn't even attempt to suppress her shudder.

"Ms. Irene and Ms. Erlene were big into hunting," Saunders said.

"Apparently they were good with a gun."

"Most people in these parts are."

She dragged her gaze away from the glassy-eyed caribou to take stock of the rest of the cabin. She could forget the deluxe-accommodations fantasy engendered by her gourmet meal.

The den and kitchen were one big room made of chinked wooden logs. A rag rug covered a large portion of the wood floor. The kitchen looked utilitarian, with appliances that appeared a few decades old and a beat-up enamel countertop that formed an "L" with the sink in the shortest part. Faded gingham cloth covered the area below the counter rather than actual cupboard doors. The faint aroma of pine cleaner hung in the air. Skye appreciated the fact that Gus and Luellen had gone out of their way to tidy up for her.

She followed Saunders to the other room with her suitcases and stopped short. Once again, Ms. Irene had apparently indulged her inner pioneer spirit. A polar bear rug covered an alarmingly large portion of the wooden floor. No IKEA knock-off here—the head and claws were all still charmingly attached. Two small nightstands flanked a double bed with a slatted pine headboard. An unframed mirror hung on one wall. And that was it. No doorway indicated a closet. No chifferobe stood in the corner. Nothing. "Where's the closet?"

"That's what Ms. Irene used." Saunders nodded toward an array of wooden pegs on one wall. "She was something of a minimalist."

"Apparently. There is running water, right?" There was obviously electricity because lights were on. At this juncture she considered herself lucky the cabin wasn't lit by whale-oil lanterns.

He winced. "For the most part."

"For the most part?"

"Well, apparently there's a little problem with the shower."

She crossed her arms over her chest. There didn't need to be any problem with the shower. "What kind of problem?"

"It's not working right now. Merrilee said Gus had

told her when they got back but there wasn't time for anyone to take care of it."

"I have to have a shower." This was the straw that broke the camel's back. Her voice escalated, along with her temper. "I can't go to bed germ and grime-ridden. I have to go to work tomorrow. How can I take care of patients looking like this?"

Saunders shrugged. "I'll see if I have time to take care of it tomorrow."

Did he not understand what dangerous ground he was treading? "Tomorrow's not soon enough. I need a shower tonight." She grabbed the overnight travel bag she always kept on the plane with her. "Let's go."

He looked at her as if she'd lost her faculties. "I'm not driving you back into town tonight."

"I'm not asking you to." She marched toward the door.

"Then where do you plan to go?" Amusement tinged his voice as he followed her.

She looked at him over her shoulder. "Do you have a working shower?"

"Yes, but—"

She cut him off. She might be stuck out in the middle of nowhere, surrounded by dead animals and crazy people, but she would not be denied the basics. They squared off at her cabin's front door. "I don't have cooties, Saunders. I need to clean up. We're out in the middle of nowhere. You have a working shower next door. I plan to avail myself of it."

"Most people ask first, Shanahan."

"Most decent people would've offered, Saunders."

"You're not going to take no for an answer, are you?"

"What's the big deal?"

"I live out here because I like my privacy, Shanahan."

"I'm not suggesting a slumber party, Saunders. I just want to clean up and then I'll be out of your hair."

He sighed heavily and opened her door. "Well, come on…"

"Your generosity is only exceeded by your graciousness." She brushed past him.

Ten feet, maybe a dozen at most, separated the two cabins. "It's close, that's for sure."

"They wanted to be able to talk to one another without leaving their front porches, so they built them separate, but close."

"I hope I don't hear you snore tonight." She must be overtired because she came precariously close to giggling at the thought.

She'd be lying up one side and down the other if she didn't admit that she was now intensely curious to see Saunders's place. And she was more than a little nervous that she was about to take her clothes off in the home of a man she felt this incredible attraction toward. But her need to shower and her curiosity outweighed her trepidation.

Saunders opened the door and stood to the side for her to enter ahead of him. His cabin was laid out identical to hers, but that's where the similarity ended. Well, the most notable difference was the lack of dead animal heads and bodies scattered around the place.

The second difference was the array of Alaskan wildlife and wilderness photographs covering the walls. Much as she was loathe to admit it, it was masculine but cozy. Saunders might eschew supposed material possessions but the chocolate-brown leather sofa with a blanket thrown over the back looked butter-soft and worn. He'd skipped the polar bear and a plain area rug in shades of green and brown covered the floor between the fireplace and the couch.

On the other side of the room, a desk with plain lines held a laptop and printer. A nice flat-screen TV sat against one wall. She'd look for the dish tomorrow because she was a hundred percent sure no one was running cable out here. But it was the photographs that really gave the room warmth and character.

"Are you the photographer, Saunders?"

"It's a hobby. The bathroom's this way."

She trailed behind him to the door wedged between the kitchen and the den, as uninspired as the one in the cabin next door—apparently Irene and Erlene had the same propensity for cooking as Skye.

The bathroom was a rectangle with a mirror and a sink—she noted Saunders seemed to be fairly tidy, thank God—a toilet, and at the opposite end of the room, a standing shower. Apparently, the twins hadn't felt the need to loll about in a tub soaking away a hard day of hunting. Oh well, it worked for her.

Saunders grabbed a towel and wash cloth off a peg.

"They're clean. Lucky for you, I have two towels and I just did laundry yesterday." It was tight quarters and her heart began to thump as he brushed past her, his scent surrounding her. "Just don't use all the hot water, Shanahan."

IF SHE'D DIED IN THERE, surely he would've heard the thunk when she fell. If this was her version of a short shower, he hated to see her idea of a long one. He'd be lucky to have hot water again by next week.

He cut her some slack. People fresh up from the lower forty-eight just didn't get the differences right away. Things they took for granted as an everyday amenity weren't always so quick to be found here. Shanahan probably lived in an apartment or a house with a huge hot-water heater. Several months a year his hot water was a rudimentary solar system. In the winter he switched to propane.

Either way, it wasn't a big system. He figured she'd be out of water about—a yelp sounded from the bathroom and he grinned—now.

He deliberately set about preparing his clothes for tomorrow morning, not that there was much to be done in that arena, but it was better than thinking about Shanahan naked in the next room with her long red hair streaming down her back, drying her long pale freckled limbs with his towel.

What was it about her that drew him to her? He'd been seeing Janice off and on for a couple of months now. Nothing serious on either side. When he was in

Juneau, they'd catch dinner or a movie and he'd often wind up spending the night. They had a good time together.

But today in the meadow, tonight in the truck with the moon slanting through, and thinking of her now wet and naked in his bathroom…there was something elemental between them. It was like some goddamned call of the wild. He sure as hell didn't feel that way when he was with Janice.

What the hell was wrong with him? For all he knew, Shanahan could have a husband and two kids somewhere back in the lower forty-eight. Or she could be engaged, all tied up with a significant other. It was really none of his business—none of his business at all.

He heard the hum of the blow-dryer and he paced the den. It was odd to have her in his cabin. Every now and again Bull would drop in or Charlie Talkeet would stop over to show off a new flute carving, but for the most part, he saw people elsewhere, not in his cabin.

Dalton was downloading photos from his camera when the bathroom door opened.

"I know you only offered under duress, but thank you. I actually feel human again—the restorative powers of a hot shower."

Glancing up, he froze. It was as if he, along with time, stood still. She, quite literally, took his breath away. Her hair was a vibrant, shimmering cloud of curls that stood out from her head and fell below her shoulders while her eyes made him feel as if he was soaring into the open sky.

She shifted from one foot to the other and tucked her hair behind one ear, which just left the delicate, pale shell of her ear contrasting against the gold-flecked red. "It's late and I'm too tired to straighten it tonight. It's uncontrollable."

"It makes me want to touch it," he said hoarsely, without weighing or measuring his words, simply giving voice to what he felt.

She swallowed, working the pale column of her throat. Her blue eyes widened. "It does?"

"Yes." He wasn't sure if he'd ever wanted anything more. He crossed the room and stopped before her. "May I?"

She hesitated and her fingers fluttered at her throat. "I…um…suppose."

Dalton reached out and caught one of those curls on his index finger. It was warm and silky and as he moved his finger, her soft hair wound around his hard, calloused flesh. "It's so soft." He bent down slightly and inhaled. "And it smells good." He couldn't discern scents—all he knew was that she smelled clean, expensive, arousing. It was erotically intimate to have her hair wrapped around his finger.

He was mesmerized, bewitched. He bent his head lower and wisps of fragrant silk teased against his skin. The delicate shell of her ear was mere inches from his mouth, the skin so translucent he imagined he could see the trace of fine veins.

Or, sweet God, that cloud of soft red curls spread out over his white pillow…

"Saunders." Her voice was a husky whisper. "I think I should go."

As if he'd been freed from a spell, he snapped his head up and pulled his hand away from her hair. He wasn't sure what had just happened but it had been potent. He'd been on the verge of making a total fool of himself over this woman.

Wouldn't that make an amusing tale for her to regale her colleagues with in a couple of weeks—how she'd nearly been mauled by an Alaskan on her first day here.

"Okay, Doc." He turned and headed for the cabin door. "We need to head out around six-fifteen in the morning." She followed him. "I'll be sure to take care of your shower sometime tomorrow."

He held the door for her. When she brushed past him, he felt himself unhinging all over again. "Thank you."

It was dark out, except for the moonlight slanting across the quiet lake, picking out the worn path between the two cabins. A loon's cry shattered the silence and Shanahan stopped, spinning around. Momentum carried him into her and he automatically reached out to steady himself.

"Easy. That's just a loon."

"Oh." But she didn't step away. Instead her fingers curled around his biceps and her eyes were luminous in the moonlight. Her lips parted and Dalton did something he never did—he reacted without considering the consequences, without weighing the pros and cons. He did what he'd wanted to do from the first moment he'd laid eyes on her.

Dalton bent his head, threaded his fingers through her silken cloud of hair, and in the crisp moonlit Alaskan night, he staked his claim on Dr. Skye Shanahan.

6

ABSOLUTE, UTTER BLISS. That was what it was like to stand in the cold northern wilderness and kiss a veritable stranger beneath a brilliant starry sky. His lips were warm, firm, tender and certain, but not demanding. It was perhaps the most perfect kiss she'd ever had. And quite possibly the worst thing to ever happen to her.

As if perhaps the same thought had filtered through his brain, she and Saunders pulled away from one another.

Silently she turned and continued along the path to her cabin. Saunders followed without saying a word, for which she supposed she was thankful. She wasn't sure whether she was grateful he didn't spoil what had been a perfect moment or if she would have preferred he had, so the moment would no longer be perfect.

Saunders stopped at the bottom step leading up to the porch. "We need to leave at 6:15. Call me if you need anything in the meantime."

"Call you? What? Should I open the window and yell?"

Even with his face in the shadows, she saw a flash of a smile. "Better than that. Did you ever play that game as a kid where you connected two cups with a piece of string, making a telephone of sorts? What's here is a little more sophisticated than that, but it's the same idea. Irene and Erlene knew they had to back one another up. There's a device in each room that puts you in touch with my cabin. Call me if you need anything. Within reason, of course."

She opened the door, the lamp light from inside spilling across the boards of the front porch. She turned to face him, steadying herself on the rough-hewn door frame. The interior light stopped just short of the front step where he stood cloaked in the shadows. The scent of evergreen rode on the crisp night air. Otherwise, all was still, except for her still-uneven heartbeat echoing in her ears. "I'll try to keep all my unreasonable requests to myself."

"Much appreciated."

He turned on his heel and she closed her front door, dropping the latch into place and turning the lock. She'd almost asked about bears, but the truth of the matter was she'd really rather not know. She was pretty sure they'd begun to hibernate, but pretty sure wasn't certain. Locking the door seemed like a good plan.

Exhaustion swamped her. She still needed to unpack and organize but it had been a full, eventful day and given what there was to do in Good Riddance, which was absolutely nothing, she'd have plenty of time for that tomorrow after work.

Leaving the lamp still burning, she crossed the wood floor on unsteady legs to the bedroom. She put her bag in the corner, beside the rest of her luggage. It might not be the most ecological decision to leave the den light on, but she liked the idea of a giant nightlight on the other side of her bedroom door.

She set her travel alarm and crawled in between sheets which, while not luxurious, felt and smelled clean. Lace curtains, something of a juxtaposition considering all the mounted animal heads and bodies in the other room and the polar bear stretched out on the floor at the foot of the bed, hung across the lower half of the bedroom window. Her bedroom window faced Saunders's.

She smiled to herself at the quirkiness of the two sisters. "They couldn't stand to live together but they didn't want to live apart," he'd said. She could well imagine the two of them lying in their respective beds, windows open in the summertime, talking to one another until they both drifted off to sleep.

Across the way, the light was on in Saunders's bedroom and she could see his silhouette moving about. He might not be naked, but there was no doubt he was wearing far less clothing now than he had been five minutes ago. Through the curtain, she could see the outline of muscular arms and trim waist. She closed her eyes, not so much out of a sense of propriety as self-preservation.

That kiss… She felt all warm and melting inside.

Thinking about that kiss was just a bad idea any way she looked at it, ranking right up there with watching a stripped-down silhouette.

She needed to be practical. Practical meant finding the device he'd mentioned in case of an emergency. There was no excuse for not being prepared. She didn't have to turn on the light. With the open panes at the top and the sheer lace at the bottom, the moon served as a generous night light.

On the nightstand next to the bed was what appeared to be an old-fashioned handset. She picked it up. It was strange. She was conditioned to hear a dial tone but there was only silence on the other end. So she nearly jumped out of her skin when Saunders's voice came over the other end. "What do you need, Doc?"

There was no denying the sheer sexiness of the man and his voice. He radiated a sensuality that was all the more devastating because it was just a natural state of being for him. He didn't even have to try. "Um, nothing. I was just checking out this device. But I didn't dial you or anything. I just picked it up."

"You don't have to dial. It automatically rings on the other end. Hang up and I'll show you."

She replaced the receiver and within a few seconds a sharp, impossible-to-miss noise rang from the device. She picked up. "Hello." It was an automatic response.

Saunders laughed on the other end. "It's me, Shanahan."

He had a nice laugh that made her melt a little deeper into the mattress. "Right."

"Okay. So that's how it works. No need to dial anything, you just pick up and wait."

"Got it."

"Are you okay?"

Considering he'd found her a pain in the ass all afternoon—yes, she had enough self-awareness and people skills to know she'd exasperated him—it was nice of him to ask. And perhaps she hadn't been at her most tolerant today.

"I'm fine. Thanks for asking. I just wanted to know how this worked before I went to sleep, you know, in case there was an emergency in the middle of the night."

"Do you need anything before you go to bed?"

"I'm already in bed."

"Oh. I see."

There was something very, very nice about hearing his voice on the other end of the line while she was snuggled beneath clean sheets and a couple of hand-sewn quilts. Which just went to show how terribly exhausted she had to be. After all, she didn't even like him. But she must be over the edge because she wriggled a little deeper under the covers and said, "You can't actually see, can you?" God help her, she needed her head examined. There was actually a flirtatious note in her voice.

"Hate to tell you, Shanahan, but I've got a bird's-eye view right into your bedroom."

The not-so-proper Irish chick in her responded to the husky note in his voice. Dr. Shanahan was off-duty.

She shifted restlessly beneath the covers, her body feeling too tight for her own skin, seeking a release she hadn't felt in far too long. The kind of satisfaction that didn't come from her own hand or the purr of a battery-powered vibrator but from the brush of a masculine hand across feminine flesh, the whisper of a man's lips against her own. Her breath felt trapped in her chest at the notion that he could see into her bedroom. "I don't believe you."

"Why?" His voice seemed to scrape across her skin, leaving the prickle of goose flesh in its wake. "Are you afraid of what I might see?"

Oh, this was dangerous territory, especially considering that earlier kiss. But lying in bed flirting with Dalton Saunders was too tempting to resist. She was the moth and, God help her, from the moment she laid eyes on him, he was the flame. "Not a bit—I just don't want to be staying next to a peeping Tom."

"But my first name is Dalton, not Tom. And I can tell you exactly what you're wearing." He paused. "It looks like flannel, a high-necked gown with a buttoned-up collar and long sleeves. Starched."

She gasped and strove for the perfect blend of sincerity, horror and outrage. "Oh, my, God. You can see in. I want that window boarded up tomorrow even before the shower is repaired."

"You're serious? That's what you're wearing?"

Ha. She had him. "Nice try, Saunders, but you even knew about the buttoned-up collar."

"I swear, I didn't really look, Shanahan."

"I don't believe you," This was too much fun and she couldn't believe she actually had him going. He definitely had her going. Moisture gathered between her thighs and dampened her panties. "I don't believe you for a minute. There's no way you could have known all of that if you hadn't looked. This is an outrage."

"But, I—"

She couldn't stand it anymore. "Got you, Saunders."

There was a stunned silence on the other end and then he started laughing. "You got me good, Shanahan. You'll pay for that."

She knew precisely the price she'd like for him to exact. If that's what kissing him had been like, then… "Idle threats don't scare me."

"When you least expect it…"

She smiled softly into the phone-like device. "My guard is never down, Saunders."

"Never? That sounds like a challenge."

"Good night, Saunders."

"Shanahan?"

"Yeah?"

He cleared his throat but his voice still came out a little husky. "What are you wearing?"

"'Night, Saunders. I'll see you in the morning."

She replaced the receiver and rolled onto her side. She had a very clear view of him outlined in the window. Her entire body tightened at the thought of trailing her fingers and her mouth over his angles and planes. Most of the time she viewed the human body with a medical objectivity. That was so gone. She was view-ing Saunders's body strictly with a woman's intention of appreciating a man.

They were worlds apart. He was all wrong for her. Nonetheless, the ache he engendered between her thighs was all too real. She lightly brushed her fingers over the crotch of her damp panties and bit back a sigh. She could bring herself relief but that wasn't what Skye wanted.

She resolutely rolled to her other side. With a good night's sleep behind her, perhaps this foolish attraction to Dalton Saunders would dissipate. And if not, she would ruthlessly bury it.

THE FOLLOWING MORNING, Dalton wasn't surprised at all that the woman with the cloud of red curls who'd flirted with him over the call wire had disappeared. If he was even remotely prone to hallucination, he might've thought he'd imagined the whole thing, but she'd been no fanciful dream last night.

Just as the prim professional with straightened hair pulled back into a neat roll at the back of her head, black-rimmed glasses firmly seated on her nose, neat pantsuit and doctor's bag waiting on her front porch in the still, dark morning was no figment of his imagina-tion, either.

His restless night had been real, too. What the hell was wrong with him? He'd more than learned his lesson with Lauren, so why was he so caught up in Dr. Skye Shanahan when she so obviously wasn't a woman who would appreciate his lifestyle? He was thinking with the wrong head, that's what the problem was. It wasn't usually a problem for him, but he couldn't seem to move beyond it now.

"Morning, Doc. Ready?"

Regardless of her professional demeanor, last night's conversation and kiss stretched between them like a taut fishing line. For one brief second of insanity, the notion of taking her into his arms for a good-morning kiss crossed his mind. He could've sworn the flicker in her eyes said she'd thought the same thing. Luckily, however, sanity prevailed.

"Morning, Saunders. I'm ready to go when you are."

They walked in silence to the truck. She was looking all around the cabins, though she asked no questions or made any comments. It had been dark last night when they'd arrived and while they wouldn't see the sunrise for a couple of hours, the pre-dawn darkness was different.

Dalton opened the truck door for her. "It's called Shadow Lake because with the mountains on three sides of the lake, at least one part of the water is in a mountain's shadow almost all of the time."

He inhaled the fresh clean scent of the air as he rounded the truck to his side. While he loved the longer days of summer, there was something about fall, the urgency to take in everything before the long, cold days of winter. He climbed into the driver's seat and started the engine.

Her eyes slightly narrowed, Shanahan studied the

area outside the window. "It's lovely…in an isolated, wild kind of way." She fixed those amazing eyes of hers on him. "Don't you ever get lonely out here?"

"I'm comfortable in my own skin."

"So am I. But I enjoy the company of other people, nonetheless."

He was honest with her. "Sometimes it does get a little isolated, especially since Ms. Irene passed. I didn't realize how much I'd grown used to having her next door until she was gone."

"She sounds like quite a character."

He put the truck in gear and headed toward the road. "That she was. She and Erlene were two of a kind."

"She didn't have any family that wanted to move into her cabin?"

"All of their family was back East. They had the occasional niece and nephew visit but none of their relatives loved Alaska the way those two women did." He decided he might as well tell her the whole truth. It wasn't as if it was a state secret and if someone mentioned it in town, it would look as if he had been trying to hide it. "Ms. Irene left all of her money to her nieces and her nephews, but she left Shadow Lake to me."

Surprise flickered across her face. "That was very generous."

"Yes, it was. I didn't have a clue until Irene's attorney got in touch with me." He still wasn't sure how he felt about it. It wasn't a responsibility he particularly wanted. "I assumed the family would take over Shadow Lake and most likely sell it. I'd already been planning to move back to town." As much as he'd grown to care for Ms. Irene, he'd been looking forward to being around more people. But how could he abandon a property she and her sister had loved, a property she'd entrusted to him? It had been generous, but it had come with strings he hadn't particularly wanted.

"So, how big is Shadow Lake?"

"The property or the lake itself?"

"The property."

"Eighteen."

"Eighteen acres or eighteen square miles?"

He was almost embarrassed to tell her. "Alaska's vast. Out here, things are measured in larger terms. Eighteen is eighteen-hundred. One thousand eight hundred acres."

"A woman you lived next to for six years left you eighteen hundred acres and two cabins? I'm thinking that went over with her family like a lead balloon."

"That about sums it up."

A small frown bisected her forehead. "So, I'm actually staying in your cabin."

"Technically, yes."

"Thank you, then."

"Don't mention it. The clinic closes at five. How about I pick you up around five-thirty? That should give you time to finish up with the last patient."

"Would you mind if I met you at Gus's around six-thirty so I could grab dinner? I'm not much of a cook and I'd just as soon eat there instead of buying groceries and cooking for myself at the cabin. Even if I was a decent cook, I couldn't begin to turn out anything that remotely touched Gus's."

He grinned. "I was going to pick you up at five-thirty and suggest a stop at Gus's on the way home. By the way, I wanted to give you fair warning, you're going to be slammed today."

"How do you know?"

She obviously didn't have a clue. "We don't get a lot of strangers in town. Doc Morrow hasn't taken a vacation in two years. People have been saving up non-emergency issues so they could have a legitimate reason to see the visiting doctor. And now that word's out that you're a pretty young woman, they'll really line up at your door. You aren't married, right?"

"No."

"Did Merrilee ask you last night?"

"Well, yes."

He almost felt sorry for her. She'd be lucky if she had time to breathe today. "Honey, they won't just be lined up at the door, they'll be lined down the sidewalk."

She shot him a skeptical look. "It's a medical center, not a dating service."

"It won't matter. You'll need to be prepared when you go to Gus's tonight for dinner, too. You'll have so many drinks sent your way, I'd have to carry you out of the bar if you drank half of them."

Her blue eyes widened at the corner. "You're not kidding, are you?"

"Not a bit. You'll be a hot commodity in Good Riddance, Doc. You'll draw men from five hundred miles away." The idea had his gut clenching and his hand tightening on the steering wheel. "Who knows, you might even find the man of your dreams up here, Shanahan."

Disdain replaced her skepticism. "Saunders, you really do possess the most twisted sense of humor."

Her reaction didn't surprise him—he'd had her number from the beginning. Still it felt a bit like a slap in the face. "Stranger things have happened."

"I have a requirements list—"

"Why does that not surprise me?"

She ignored his interjection. "And in the top ten of those requirements is a no-wilderness qualifier. Feel free to put that out there."

He shook his head and forced a laugh as he turned onto Main Street, making a right next to Curl's Taxidermy and Salon. "You don't understand the men in this state. It's a different breed that comes to Alaska. Most of them would simply see that list as a challenge."

"A challenge?"

He tried to explain. "Yeah, to prove you wrong."

"Well, if the grapevine's that active, put out the word that they'll be wasting their time."

He braked for Elaine Yarber and her three sled dogs to cross, raising a hand in greeting. "Then all the lesbians will be lining up. We've got our fair share of them, too."

Skye looked as if she was torn between amusement and exasperation. "For sweet pity's sake, Saunders. I'm here to fill in for another medical professional. Can't you stop this before it turns into a three-ring circus?"

"Hey, don't shoot the messenger. I'm just trying to prepare you for what to expect."

"Can't you assure them that I'm not a lesbian but I'm not interested?"

He was sorry he'd even brought it up. It would've been best to simply stay out of it. "Why would I want to compromise my reputation that way?"

She narrowed her eyes across the way at him. "Compromise your reputation? How so?"

This wasn't going to make the Doc a happy camper. "If I put out the word for everyone to back off, they'll all think I'm staking my claim. They'll think you and I have hooked up."

She spluttered in the seat next to him—honest-to-God spluttered—and he grinned at her. "Hey, you asked, Shanahan. I'm simply explaining the Alaskan male psyche."

He pulled up in front of the weathered building that served as Doc Morrow's office.

"Dating me would compromise your reputation, Saunders?" She opened the door and stepped out, narrowing her eyes at him. "You should be so lucky."

She slammed the door extra hard.

"Have a nice day," he yelled after her. Good, that was Shanahan's payback for keeping him awake half the damn night imagining her wearing everything from silk pajamas to a lacy teddy to nothing at all.

He whistled a tune beneath his breath as he pointed

his truck in the direction of the airfield. Certainly no one could accuse Skye Shanahan of being boring. She'd already shaken a lot of things up—including him!

7

"THAT'S IT, DR. SKYE. All done for the day," Nelson said, crossing the hall from one of the two exam rooms to her office.

Skye looked up from chart where she was making notes and motioned for Nelson to sit in the chair on the opposite side of her desk. "It was an interesting day, that's for sure."

Interesting being the definitive word. Certainly an interesting array of patients with an interesting assortment of ailments. And the office itself was…different. She'd wager her pay that none of the equipment in the office was newer than fifteen years old. And Nelson had confirmed the paint had come from an Army surplus, which explained why all the rooms were a charming Army green. However, the most startling decorative touch was the assortment of sunflowers, in varying sizes, painted in bright yellow all over the walls. Nelson had related Dr. Morrow's philosophy that a positive attitude went far in helping a patient heal. Yellow and red industrial tile, yet another surplus item, covered the floor. The entire office was a far cry from the tasteful, interior designer decorated medical offices that were part of Skye's experience.

However, despite the outdated equipment and the funky décor, she'd surprisingly enjoyed her day. It was as if she'd had to travel more than four thousand miles to be reminded that she'd become a doctor because, at the end of the day, healing was what she was called to do.

"Thank you, Nelson, for everything. You were a life saver today." And he had been. The tall, quiet man had been efficient, seeming to almost anticipate her needs before *she* knew what they were.

His smile thanked her acknowledgment as he settled into the chair. "No problem. You are equally busy tomorrow, and the day after, as well."

They'd been swamped. "You did a great job of sorting by triage."

He smiled and she absently wondered why Nelson's smile didn't send a shiver through her like…well, some other people's smiles did. Nelson was quite handsome with long black hair, wonderful bone structure, and obsidian black eyes. He was intelligent, organized and easy to be around. And he brewed a stellar cup of coffee. But he didn't send even a faint tingle chasing down her spine. That was good, she supposed, since they were working together, but rather confounding since all she'd done was tingle around Saunders.

"Many of the guys just wanted a chance to meet you."

He flashed a conspiratorial smile. "They'll all crowd Gus's tonight, hoping you'll show up."

She was tired and the notion of running a gauntlet of men at Gus's simply increased her exhaustion. The time zone change was really playing havoc with her nerves. Leaning back in the rickety office chair old enough to qualify as an antique, she sighed. "How long will this last?"

"Oh, probably until you leave," he said with an almost apologetic smile.

"It'll be the same at Gus's?" She knew even before she asked, but hope sprang eternal.

"It'll be the same anywhere in Good Riddance."

Good grief. She bowed her head, resting her forehead against her palm. "Saunders was right." Good Lord but it was galling to admit.

"I was right about what?"

Speaking of the devil… Skye snapped her head up as Saunders walked into her office. She hadn't even heard the front door open.

"Hi, Dalton," Nelson said.

"What's up, Nelson?" Saunders propped himself against the wall and the ridiculous thought passed through her overly tired brain that he looked very handsome in his jacket and cap.

"All the men showed up today to see Dr. Skye," Nelson said. "Bard Cannon came all the way from Snowshoe Pass."

Saunders whistled under his breath. Skye didn't even

want to know how far away Snowshoe Pass was. "Poor devil. His wife died last year."

"Yep, and he lost his dog a few months ago." Nelson looked more mournful about the dog than the wife.

"He's had a run of bad luck. No doubt about it," Saunders said. "Mind if I finish it up?" He nodded toward the last cup of coffee in the carafe on her credenza. Nelson kept a pot going for the patients in the waiting room but he'd also had a fresh pot in her office just for her this morning. And after lunch, he'd brewed what he called an afternoon pick-me-up.

"Help yourself," she said. "Although it's several hours old at this point."

Saunders was already pouring before she finished speaking. "I sort of like it after it's been sitting a while." He took a swallow and hoisted his cup in Nelson's direction. "Good stuff. So, Bard will be in town for a while?" he asked, swinging back to what they'd been discussing.

Nelson, who possessed a stillness about him that was very soothing, nodded. "He'll be at Gus's. He came in today with a sore throat but I told him Dr. Skye couldn't see him until tomorrow afternoon."

She cleared her throat. "Patient confidentiality, Nelson."

"He stated his ailment in front of twenty people sitting in the waiting room, Dr. Skye."

True enough. No nifty glass wall divided any portion of the waiting room and front office. It was just one big open space, one that had been very crowded today.

Saunders regarded her over the coffee mug rim, as if sizing her up. "You ready for Gus's, Doc?"

She looked from Saunders to Nelson and back to the bush pilot. "You two are serious, aren't you?"

"As a heart attack, if you'll pardon the expression. Hey, it's like I told you. You're single and not bad looking. They're going to be like wolves on a fresh caribou carcass."

Not bad looking? What happened to her being pretty this morning? "Thank you for that poetic analogy."

He simply smirked as he upended the coffee cup.

"Dalton could put his arm around you when you walk in and they'd leave you alone," Nelson said.

What about him? Couldn't Nelson put his arm around her with the same results?

"It wouldn't look good if it was me because we work together and that would be unprofessional," he added.

It was a little unnerving how Nelson seemed to read her mind.

"Besides, everyone knows I can't date white women. It's forbidden for the son of a shaman. Anyway, the Sis-nukets haven't had much luck with mixed marriages."

"Remember meeting Clint yesterday at the air strip?" Saunders said. "His mother is white and she couldn't adjust to the culture."

Apparently everyone's private business was public knowledge in this place, which was a difficult concept to embrace given her locked-up family history. Although she fully suspected there were still plenty of secrets in this town. No one lived this transparent. It simply wasn't human nature.

"This conversation is ridiculous. I'm sure it's not going to be like wolves on a caribou carcass."

The two men exchanged a she'll-see-soon-enough look. "They'll come to your cabin," Nelson said, sending her a mournful look. "Bard brought his guitar. He said he's planning to serenade you."

"That's—" She hesitated, trying to decide between preposterous and arcane.

"Good Riddance, Alaska," Saunders jumped in with a smirk. "Where the women are scarce and most of the men are desperate."

"Thanks, Saunders," she said.

He shrugged. "I can stake a claim at Gus's if you want me to."

The idea set her pulse racing. "You make it sound as if I'm a gold mine."

"Most men here would consider you the next best thing."

Did he consider her the next best thing? Could she handle being "claimed" by a man who already sent her into a tailspin with little more than a kiss?

"Okay, hypothetically, say you stake your claim. What about poachers?" She couldn't believe she was even asking such a thing, giving this nonsense more than a passing nod.

"There's a code of honor that goes back to the gold rush days," Nelson said. "Once a claim is staked, everyone respects it."

This time she did hear the door open. "Evening everyone," Merrilee said as she came in wearing mukluks—a fur-lined, animal-skin boot—a mid-calf denim skirt and a lavender and pink flannel shirt trimmed in ecru lace beneath a down coat.

Nelson rose, offering Merrilee his chair. The other chair had been moved out to the waiting room earlier in the day. "Have a seat."

Merrilee waved him back down. "No. I'm fine."

"I've got to rinse out the coffee maker anyway."

"Oh, okay," she said, slipping off her coat and perching on the edge of the seat. "You about done for the evening, Dr. Skye? Gus's is packed—the place is busting at the seams with folks." Merrilee beamed. "You're good for business. Gus said she's sold more drinks today than she has in weeks. There's already a dozen bought up for you."

The pipe clanged overhead and Skye jumped as Nelson ran water in the sink in the next room. The plumbing left a lot to be desired. Every time water ran, which meant everything from hand washing to the toilet flushing, the pipes clanged. It was quite disconcerting. But clanging pipes weren't nearly as disconcerting as the topic at hand.

Not that she'd particularly doubted Nelson and Saunders after the first few minutes, but Merrilee's assessment really brought it home to her. Fine. It would obviously be easier to set up some crazy semblance of an alliance with Saunders than to be hit on relentlessly for the next two weeks. The whole thing was madness.

And here she was joining in the insanity. She looked at Saunders.

There was a flicker of acknowledgment in his eyes that sent a shiver down Skye's spine. Feeling as if she was doing something totally out of character, she took a step toward him. He bridged the distance and took Skye's hand, curling his fingers in between hers. "I'm afraid those boys are about to be sorely disappointed, Merrilee. Because I beat them to the punch. My mama didn't raise a fool." He brought her hand to his mouth and pressed a kiss against the back.

Merrilee looked from Saunders to Skye, who tried to smile normally. But it was hard when her heart was thumping against her ribs ninety to nothing from the sensations of having his hand engulfing hers and his warm lips branding her hand. "Well, well, well, that didn't take long, but that's the way things happen here. I can't say I'm surprised. I thought there was some chemistry there yesterday." Merrilee winked at her. "Wise choice, Dr. Skye. They don't come any finer than Dalton."

Obviously Merrilee didn't know Saunders had done hard time.

"I knew the minute I saw her," Saunders said, giving Skye a besotted look, although she could see the glimmer of amusement in his eyes. Even though she knew it was a charade, her breath caught in her throat. Beneath the play-acting and his humor, there was no mistaking the lambent heat in his eyes.

"I was so impressed with the way Saunders handled

my luggage," Skye said. Hey, it was the best she could come up with.

"Ready for a drink and some dinner, Shanahan?"

A knowing smile tilted the corners of Merrilee's mouth as she stood and slipped her coat back on. "If y'all want to convince the boys over at Gus's, you might want to get on a first-name basis. Y'all had me going up till that point."

"Merrilee has a point," Nelson said, returning the clean carafe back to the stand.

Merrilee cocked her head to one side, tapping her index finger against her cheek. "You might want to exchange a kiss or two after Nelson and I skedaddle. It's always obvious when two people have kissed."

Nelson nodded, shrugging into his coat. "She's right."

Skye hadn't signed on for that. She turned to Nelson. "You said all he had to do was put his arm around me." She was already skating on thin ice, considering how she reacted every time she was around him. But if they started kissing…

"That *is* all he has to do. But you won't have to convince anybody if you kiss," Nelson said. "There's something about the isolation here that makes people more tuned into things like that."

"Absolutely," Merrilee seconded. She and Nelson turned toward the door. "We'll see you at Gus's in a few minutes." She rubbed her hands together in anticipation. "This is going to be better than whatever's playing on satellite TV tonight."

The front door closed behind them, leaving Skye alone with Saunders, her fingers still entwined with his.

She had a sudden flash of insight that while the rest of the wolves might be kept at bay, she'd just signed on with the alpha.

"I'M NOT GOING TO bite…Skye," Dalton said, trying to put her at ease. She looked as if she'd just seen something terrifying and he wasn't that bad of a guy to look at, he didn't think. "Merrilee and Nelson will lay the groundwork before we get there. But that means everyone is going to be watching extra-close when we walk in."

She tried to disentangle her hand but he held fast to it. "I suppose Nelson's right."

He wouldn't understand women, or at least this one, if he lived to be a hundred. She'd seemed to enjoy kissing him well enough last night. "Your obvious reluctance is a real ego booster, Shanahan."

"Skye," she corrected. "And what? You want to kiss me? You're the one who said it would ruin your reputation this morning."

Did he want to kiss her? If she only knew. She was like every man's fantasy with her white coat, and those black-rimmed glasses, her hair all prim and tidy. The female mind was an ongoing mystery. Didn't she have any idea what a turn-on she was, especially now that he knew how her hair looked loose and wild?

"Well, I thought about it on my flight to Sitka and

back today and it's just the gallant thing to do." It was true enough that kissing her, among other things, had occupied quite a bit of his thoughts today.

"A noble sacrifice," she said, her gaze flickering to his mouth.

That one look fired through him. Dalton closed the gap between them until they were almost touching. He braced one hand on the wall behind her. "And yeah. I do want to kiss you again."

He couldn't read the expression in her eyes. "Then let's get on with it, Saunders." She cupped the back of his neck in her hand.

"Dalton."

"Dalton." Her fingers tightened slightly against his skin and heat coiled inside him at her simple touch. "This is the craziest thing I've ever done."

He released her hand and traced her jaw line with one finger. Her skin was as soft and warm as a fine flannel. "Honey, if *this* is the craziest thing you've ever done, we've got to work on you."

Her lips parted and he outlined her lower lip with his fingertip, her breath warm against his digit. "You're virtually a stranger."

"There's one way to remedy that." And he was going to kiss her again before she talked herself out of it.

Her wariness came through in the way her lips met his. Dalton explored, teased. By the time this kiss was over, they wouldn't be strangers.

Then she was kissing him back with curiosity, with eagerness and he forgot that they had a lie to pull off.

What he wanted to do was pull her close and hard against him. But if he pushed too hard too fast, he had a feeling she'd run like hell in the other direction. He stepped back. "You're a hell of a kisser, Doc."

"I am? I mean, I am. And you're not too bad, either."

"Kissing you almost makes up for your other shortcomings," he said, teasing her.

"I wish I could say the same," she shot back, on an equally teasing note.

He laughed and grabbed her hand. "C'mon. We don't want your waiting suitors to slam back so many drinks that they're drunk when they find out the crushing news. Then there'd likely be a fight and Gus frowns on fighting."

She looked at him suspiciously. "I'm never quite sure when you're serious or when you're telling me some tall tale."

He grinned. "It doesn't happen often, but it has happened. Too much booze, too much testosterone and tempers flare. Gus just invites them to take it outside."

"Hold on." She exchanged her white lab coat for a wool overcoat and gloves. "Okay."

They stepped outside. The early evening air held a definite bite. He liked it like this, however. "Take a minute to look at that sky. You don't see that in Atlanta."

She tilted her head back. "As trite as it sounds, it looks like you can almost reach out and touch the stars." She looked at him. "And no, we don't have night skies like this in Atlanta. Then again, I don't need anyone to claim me to fend off the other men there either."

Across the street, Donna stuck her head out the door. "You headed to Gus's?"

"On the way now," Dalton yelled back.

"I just finished rebuilding a carburetor. I'll be there as soon as I clean up."

"See you then," Skye said with a wave. "She came over today. She's nice."

Dalton offered his arm and she took it. Together they moved in the direction of Gus's.

"So how is it that none of those Southern men have snapped you up yet?"

They dodged a couple of kids playing kickball on the sidewalk in front of the dry-goods store and local shipping center/post office. "I've been just a little bit busy, Saunders, between med school, residency and working."

"And then there's the list," he said. Part of him was curious as hell as to the exact requirements on that list and the other part of him preferred not to know, especially as it had no bearing on him personally.

"Yes, there is the list."

He pulled her closer to his side and she stiffened. He leaned down and murmured in her ear for the benefit of anyone who might be watching or listening. "This is only going to work if you don't look like you're ready to run a country mile…Skye."

A small smile played about her mouth. "It'll be even more of a disaster if I attempt gazing at you adoringly. It's just not my thing."

Dalton laughed at her self-professed limitations.

"I don't think you could, even if you wanted to. How about aiming for something less than your usual death-glare?"

"Overwhelmingly charming, as usual, Dalton," she said, more teasing than biting.

"I try. Now let's go grind some hopes beneath your heel. That should bring a natural smile to your face."

8

SKYE PASTED ON A SMILE as Saunders—whoa, she'd better think of him as Dalton or she'd slip up for sure—pushed open the outer door to Gus's. It sounded packed if the cacophony of voices and music was anything to go by. They walked through the second door, into the large room that served as dining room, bar and general pool hall.

As if someone had pushed a mute button, the room went dead quiet except for the radio, which continued to play an Ella Fitzgerald tune. Every eye in the establishment trained on them.

Gus broke the silence. "Evening Dalton, Dr. Skye."

"Hello," Skye said, training her smile on Gus while her knees shook ever so slightly. She had no trouble walking into a roomful of patients but this was something else. She hated being the center of this kind of attention.

Dalton offered up an easy smile. "Evening, Gus. Think you could set us up with a table for two?"

The place was packed—obviously no table for two was available—but his request sent a message loud and clear.

"Son of a gun," someone muttered over in the general direction of the pool table.

"Saunders," another disgruntled male voice chimed in. "Wouldn't you know?"

Then the room was just as noisy as it had been. Skye did her darnedest not to actually look at any of the men. She didn't know how seriously to take Saunders's mention of a bar fight.

While she'd always known she possessed neither the face nor figure to launch a thousand ships, this was Alaska, where the men were apparently desperate. She didn't want to be responsible for inciting a riot, as crazy as that notion seemed. Thank God her sister hadn't shown up. The men would've truly lost their minds— what little bit they apparently had.

Her eyes gleaming shrewdly, Gus bustled over with her ready smile. They hadn't fooled her for a moment but she wouldn't give them away. "How would you feel about sharing a booth with Nelson?"

"Great," Skye said, leaping at the opportunity not to have dinner alone with Dalton. Besides, it would give her a chance to find out more about both men. She'd been so busy today after Nelson's initial tour of the office and briefing for the day, there'd been very little opportunity for any type of conversation. She was curious about the cultural constraints that made it taboo for him to date non-native women. Not that she was interested, other than cultural curiosity.

"Works for me," Dalton said.

They followed Gus to the booths that overlooked Main Street to the right of the bar. "Merrilee said you'd be over shortly. Here you go."

The dark-haired man who'd been in the air strip office the previous night slid out of the opposite side of the booth from Nelson. She was pretty sure she remembered that he was Nelson's cousin, Clint—some type of expedition leader or guide.

He nodded. "Dr. Skye, Dalton."

"Clint," Dalton greeted him. "Don't leave just because we got here."

"I was just on my way out anyway. Dr. Yamaguchi wants to get an early start tomorrow. He's a biologist in from Tokyo," he explained to Skye. "He's here to gather research specimens. Dalton flew him in this afternoon."

"Oh, I see. That should be interesting."

Clint nodded and grinned. "I'm always happiest knocking around in the wilderness. Enjoy your dinner." He looked at his cousin. "Drop by anytime to pick up that book."

"Will do."

Of course she and Dalton had to share a side. It would've blown the entire claim-staking act had she elected to sit next to Nelson. Dalton helped her off with her coat and waited on her to slide in first, then followed. Prison felon or not, he had manners even her mother couldn't fault—except her mother would never, ever get past the prison record in the first place. Not that it mattered—Dalton Saunders would never cross her mother's path.

Maybe all the libidinous energy in town was getting to her. Back in her office she hadn't wanted the kissing to end. And now it was as if she was overly warm with Dalton's body heat next to hers, the brush of his arm against hers, the press of his thigh against her thigh.

Gus showed up with two sets of silverware wrapped in napkins. "What can I get you to drink? You've got over a dozen drinks lined up on tabs at the bar." She pushed her dark hair behind one ear with a smile. "And dinner's on the house."

"You can't keep feeding me for free," Skye protested. "By the way, breakfast was wonderful. I'd like to stop by in the morning and pick it up to go but only if you let me pay for it."

Gus held up a stilling hand. "You can pay for it tomorrow morning if you insist, but tonight is on the house." She leaned in conspiratorially, in much the same manner as her aunt, Merrilee. "You're the biggest draw I've had in a long time. You've been a cash cow."

Her grin proved contagious. Skye laughed and smiled back, shaking her head. "Great. First I'm a caribou carcass and now I'm a cash cow." They all laughed and she realized it had been far too long since she'd shared a moment like this. Even though these people had all been strangers a day ago, she felt oddly relaxed and at ease with them now. "A glass of white wine would be lovely."

"Chardonnay, pinot grigio or Riesling?"

"Chardonnay."

"Dalton?"

He ordered a beer she'd never heard of, one that sounded like a local micro-brew.

No sooner had Gus left than a tall lanky man with longish red hair and a wooly beard approached the table. "Name's Bard Cannon, ma'am. Pleased to meet you." He offered a huge, weathered hand.

Skye leaned across the table, her shoulder resting against Dalton's hard bicep as she briefly shook the other man's hand. "Nice to meet you, Mr. Cannon." She settled back on her side of the seat.

"Call me Bard, ma'am. Pretty much everyone does." He shifted his weight from foot to foot and shot Dalton an accusatory glance. "You didn't give us other fellas much of a chance there, Dalton."

Dalton slid his arm around Skye's shoulders and shot Bard a totally unrepentant look. You could stir the testosterone with a stick. "What can I say, Bard? It's not every day that a man gets to fly in a beautiful, intelligent woman."

She knew he was saying it for Bard's benefit but nonetheless Dalton's words made her glow inside. Bard simply looked mournful. "Yep. Can't say as how I blame you." He backed down quickly and looked at Nelson. "You been okay, Nelson? We didn't have a chance to catch up today."

"Just fine. I'm sorry to hear about your dog."

"Yep. Gerta was a fine dog. Well then, I'll see you tomorrow, Doc."

"I'll see you then, Mr...um, Bard."

Teddy, a pretty blonde who was Gus's second in command, brought their drinks and took their dinner order.

"Wait a sec, we need to toast," Dalton said. His gaze snared hers and she reminded herself it was for the benefit of the rest of the room. "To you arriving in Good Riddance."

"And to leaving in thirteen days and six hours," she added, with a quick smile. But somewhere inside her, she realized she wasn't as anxious to leave as she had been when she arrived. It had been an adventure. And she realized, with a sense of surprise, that she'd never had an adventure before. Her life had been ordered from the day she'd been birthed into the Shanahan family.

"You're a hard woman, Skye Shanahan," Dalton said.

Nelson smiled an enigmatic smile. "You may find you feel differently in thirteen days and six hours."

Skye clinked her glass against Nelson and Dalton's. "We'll see."

She'd just finished sipping at her wine when a mountain of a man showed up at their booth. Hello, Grand Central. Unlike Bard Cannon, this man reeked of beer and belligerence—not a particularly good combination. Dalton's arm tightened on her shoulder.

"Saunders." The man's voice was as loud as he was big.

Once again, the room quieted and everyone looked their way.

"Little John."

Obviously someone with a sense of the absurd had nicknamed him.

"You owe me an apology, Saunders."

"How do you figure that?"

"You need to apologize for horning in early." The Neanderthal glanced meaningfully at Skye.

"That's not going to happen," Dalton said.

Little John squared off. "I say it is."

Dalton withdrew his arm from her shoulders and she could feel the readiness, the alert tension radiating from him. But his demeanor was calm as he smiled and drawled, "Go ahead and hold your breath while you're waiting on it."

The rest happened so quickly she didn't catch it all. One minute Dalton was sitting next to her, then Little John threw a punch, Dalton dodged and was on his feet. Little John swung again, only this time, his ham-fist connected with Dalton's face. She winced at the sound. Quick as a flash, Dalton got in his own blow, toppling the big man to the floor and knocking him out. Blood dripped down Dalton's face.

"My word," Gus said, exasperated. "At least no furniture was broken." She motioned over to the men sitting at the bar. "A couple of you fellas, grab Little John and drag him over to that corner. Come get me when he starts to come to." She turned back to Skye, Dalton and Nelson. "I'll box up your dinners and have someone run them over to the clinic." She considered Dalton's bloody demeanor. "That eye's gonna need stitching. Good thing there's a doctor in the house."

Skye was stunned. She'd completed an E.R. rotation and seen far worse than an eye requiring sutures, but she'd never witnessed, firsthand, the violence precipitating the injury. And she'd certainly never been the catalyst for such a thing.

She held out a staying hand for Nelson. "Just stay here and enjoy your dinner. I can handle a couple of sutures on my own. No need for such idiocy to ruin your evening, as well."

Now that she was processing things, she was angry. She bundled back into her coat and gloves. On the way to the door, several of the men clapped Saunders on the back or high-fived him. Seething, she marched down the sidewalk, unlocked the clinic door, and strode back into the exam room.

Scrubbing her hands at the sink, she heard him follow her into the room. "Leave your jacket in the chair and up on the table, please." She knew she sounded terse. But she didn't care.

"What the hell is wrong with you, Shanahan? Are you ticked off because your dinner was interrupted? Or because you had to go back to work?"

She whirled around, drying her hands. "The absolute, sheer stupidity of the whole thing infuriates me."

He was a bloody mess, even though her medical

training told her it was mostly superficial. "Most women would be flattered to have two men fighting over her," he argued.

"Then most women are idiots, along with you and that Neanderthal. That fight wasn't about me. It was about stupid male pride."

"What? You thought I should've apologized to him?"

He did have a point. "Well, no."

"He took the first swing, Shanahan," he reminded her as she sponged away the blood.

"I saw, Saunders."

"I couldn't just sit there and let him beat me to a pulp, now could I?"

She drew a deep breath. "No, you couldn't. Okay, you were totally not at fault, except for coming up with this hare-brained idea in the first place."

"A busted eyebrow is a small price to pay to avoid having every male from here to Nome lined up in my driveway. Did you want Bard Cannon showing up to strum you a love song outside your window?"

"Well, no."

"Then I'd say a little gratitude wouldn't be out of line, Shanahan."

"I'd say you need to be still so I can give you a good scar when I stitch this up."

As she was suturing, she realized why she'd been so angry. Even though Saunders was annoying, and had crawled under her skin from the moment she'd met him, she couldn't bear the thought that he'd sustained an injury on her behalf. She didn't want to acknowledge it but on some level, somehow, somewhere along the way, Dalton Saunders had begun to matter to her. She forced her attention back to sewing him up.

It would've been absolute hell to be Helen of Troy.

MY GOD, THE WOMAN WAS as stubborn as they came.

She planted one hand on her hip and held the other out, palm up. "Keys, please. You are not driving. Between the numbing agent, the sutures and the bandage, you currently suffer from impaired vision."

He had visions of her grinding the gears. Plus, it was *his* truck. "What do you drive back home?"

She rolled her eyes. "Not that it has anything to do with anything, but I drive a Saab convertible. Stick shift. Now hand over your keys. I am fully capable of driving this truck and at the moment you aren't."

Clearly she wasn't going to back down. "You've got a short fuse, Shanahan." He tossed the keys to her. "Must come with the hair."

That earned him another eye roll. "No, Saunders, it comes with the company. I'm tired, I'm hungry and I'm exasperated with the behavior you people all seem to consider normal in this frozen wasteland." She slammed the door closed and cranked the truck.

"It was thirty-six degrees today. Got to hit thirty-two or below to be considered frozen." He grinned at her, even though it was an effort. "And by the way, you might want to try to look more like an angel of mercy instead of the grim reaper, at least until we get out of town." His head was beginning to throb like a bitch. It was probably just as well, after all, that she was behind the wheel. "I'll take those ibuprofen now."

"Let me guess—your head is throbbing, which is why I tried to get you to take them earlier." She shook her head. "Check your left coat pocket. I put them in there."

The pills were right where she said they'd be. He tossed two back and swallowed them without any water. "So, are you going to have to observe me when we get home?"

"Hardly."

"But I have a head injury," he said, amusing himself by baiting her. He liked the way her eyes flashed when she was exasperated.

A hint of a smile played at the corners of her mouth. "Saunders, I treated you with a dozen sutures. It wasn't brain surgery."

"Could you do that? Brain surgery?"

"Let's just say you wouldn't want me to. I'm not qualified. But my brother or my parents could. They're all neurosurgeons."

She didn't crack a smile. Damn, she was serious. Dalton whistled under his breath. "Pretty impressive. Talk about setting a standard."

She shifted smoothly and watched the highway, but her body stiffened slightly. "I'm an underachiever. I'm just a general practitioner," she admitted.

"So, only one brother?"

"No, a younger sister, too."

"Is she a brain surgeon, too?"

"No, but she's beautiful…and she married well. Her husband shares a practice with my parents and brother."

What the hell? "I have a hard time believing she's any prettier than you."

"Spare me, Saunders. There's no audience."

Didn't she have any idea how striking, how absolutely captivating she was with that porcelain skin, flaming hair, and sky blue eyes? Apparently not. "Is she as smart as you are?"

"Bridgette possesses an entire skill set outside my realm of ability. She's the ultimate hostess. There's not an awkward bone in her body. She never, ever meets a stranger and she can charm anyone. She's a real asset to Patrick's career."

Dalton wondered how many times that particular sound bite had been tossed about in front of Skye. "So, whose idea was it for you to fill in for Doc Morrow?"

"My mother's. She's friends with his mother." Her response was automatic and unguarded. He watched her self-consciousness catch up with her. "Wait a minute. Who said it was anyone's idea?"

"Just a lucky guess." He sensed a set-up. Something ridiculously akin to jealousy knotted hard and low in his gut. "I'm surprised your brother-in-law hasn't hooked you up with some wonder-boy neurosurgeon."

"Actually, Bridgette mentioned a Dr. Rancouer she wanted me to meet when I get back. And I think our mothers were hoping Dr. Morrow and I might hit it

GET 2 BOOKS

We'd like to send you two *Harlequin®* *Blaze™* novels absolutely free.
Accepting them puts you under no obligation to purchase any more bool

HOW TO GET YOUR
2 FREE BOOKS AND 2 FREE GIFTS

1. Return the reply card today, and we'll send you two *Harlequin Blaze* novels, absolutely free! We'll even pay the postage!

2. Accepting free books places you under no obligation to buy anything, ever. Whatever you decide, the free books and gifts are yours to keep, free!

3. We hope that after receiving your free books you'll want to remain a subscriber, but the choice is yours—to continue or cancel, any time at all!

EXTRA BONUS

You'll also get two free mystery gifts! (worth about $10)

FREE!

Return this card promptly to get
2 FREE BOOKS and 2 FREE GIFTS!

HARLEQUIN® *Blaze*™

YES! Please send me 2 FREE *Harlequin® Blaze*™
novels, and 2 free mystery gifts as well. I understand
I am under no obligation to purchase anything, as
explained on the back of this insert.

*About how many NEW paperback fiction books have
you purchased in the past 3 months?*

❏ 0-2	❏ 3-6	❏ 7 or more
E9Q7	E9RK	E9RV

151/351 HDL

FIRST NAME	LAST NAME

ADDRESS

APT.#	CITY

Visit us at:
www.ReaderService.com

STATE/PROV.	ZIP/POSTAL CODE

Offer limited to one per household and not applicable to series that subscriber is
currently receiving. **Your Privacy**—The Reader Service is committed to protecting your
privacy. Our Privacy Policy is available online at www.ReaderService.com or upon request
from the Reader Service. We make a portion of our mailing list available to reputable third
parties that offer products we believe may interest you. If you prefer that we not exchange
your name with other third parties, or if you wish to clarify or modify your communication
preferences, please visit us at www.ReaderService.com/consumerschoice.

◀ **DETACH AND MAIL CARD TODAY!** ▶

(H-B-10/10)

off. Little did they know he'd be gone by the time I got here."

Barry Morrow was as gay as they came. Dalton had flown him to Anchorage where he was catching a connecting flight down to San Francisco. Not that Dalton or anyone else in Good Riddance cared. But Barry Morrow was not the guy for Skye Shanahan, nor was some tight-ass named Dr. Rancouer waiting in Atlanta. He had a feeling that Dr. Rancouer would always want her hair straightened and pulled back in that sleek bun. What Dr. Skye Shanahan really needed was a man who wanted to get lost in that cloud of red curls and the depth of her sky blue eyes.

What Skye Shanahan needed was him…on a strictly temporary basis.

9

"Do you need anything else?" Skye asked as she settled Dalton on the couch with his dinner-to-go on the coffee table in front of him. She'd started a fire in the fireplace and the room was just beginning to heat up. Really, he was milking this for all it was worth. Then again, she'd always found that her male patients were the biggest babies. And she was definitely more cut out for doctoring than nursing. Her job was to fix and move on. She didn't handle the *taking care of* very well.

"You could sit down and have dinner with me," he said. "You know, make sure I don't have a seizure or something while I'm eating."

It took a second for her to realize he was simply asking her to eat with him in his funny, cryptic way. And she *was* starving. Besides, she felt much more comfortable in his cabin with the photos lining the walls than she did in the dead-animal-gallery cabin next door. And Saunders was decent company. He certainly never bored her. And his fire was already going. Well, she mentally poked fun at herself, she'd just come up with every possible justification for sharing dinner with him.

She sat down on the opposite end of the couch. "Sure. Maybe it's a good idea to keep an eye on you during dinner." He smiled, a big happy grin that said he was glad she'd decided to stay for a while. An answering smile seemed to spill from her. She'd never felt this way around anyone else. It was as if Dalton Saunders tripped emotions inside her no one else ever had. Her hand wasn't quite steady as she opened the take-out container. "How's your head?"

"Much better, thanks. It's not throbbing any longer. Will I have a scar?" He touched a finger to the edge of the bandage.

"I wish I could say no, but you'll probably have a faint mark, mainly because it bisects your eyebrow."

He grinned, looking breathtakingly, dangerously roguish with his dark hair, sexy smile, and that bandaged eye. "I don't mind a scar. It'll make a good story. Alaskans are all about telling a good story."

She snorted and fell back into something she hadn't done since she and Bridgette had been teenagers, imitating their Grandmother Shanahan with her thick Irish accent. "I'll be wagering that'd be a tall tell, that it be."

Dalton laughed, obviously delighted. "You're good at that."

"My grandmother was from the old country. She's the one who named me."

"Isle of Skye?"

"That's it. Lots of people don't get it."

"Oh, I get you." Not *it, you.* She didn't miss the distinction. His eyes seemed to hold hers and for a second she forgot to breathe, to think, to do anything other than be snared by something potent and powerful in his gaze.

She drew a deep breath, seeking equilibrium. "I was obviously swamped today. What about you? Do you have a set schedule every week or do you go day by day?"

He finished chewing and swallowed. "Sometimes it's by the hour. I had a run to Sitka today and should've been back early in the afternoon but Merrilee radioed me with an additional stop on my way back. It works though. I'm pretty flexible."

Her root vegetable gratin was delicious. "How'd you get into flying?"

"It was one of those things that always interested me as a kid. I took a ride at a country fair on a bi-plane once and I was hooked. What about medicine? When did you know you wanted to be a doctor? Or was it just a genetic predisposition?"

Maybe it's because they were so far away, or because there was no chance in hell he'd ever meet them, but Skye found it easier to step back and really look at her family. "Being a Shanahan comes with a set of rules…or perhaps a standard is more accurate. Shanahans practice medicine. I don't really remember it ever being discussed, it was simply a given, an expectation." She laughed. "I do, however, remember the moment of my big announcement. It was Thanksgiving, during my second year at Emory—"

"Med school?"

"Yeah. Med school. My brother, Patrick, had just finished his residency. Bridgette was engaged to the bright young neurosurgeon who is now my brother-in-law. Dad had just carved the turkey…and I announced I didn't want to specialize in neurosurgery." Her stomach clenched, simply remembering the expression on her parents' faces. "It wasn't well-received."

"You know what I think, Shanahan?"

It was almost alarming how much it mattered to her what Dalton Saunders thought. "What?"

"I think beneath those classic, tailored pantsuits and that carefully straightened hair beats the heart of a rebel."

He was so right, it was scary. Therefore, she stead-fastly denied it. "No, you're wrong. We Shanahans aren't made that way. Foregoing neurosurgery wasn't an act of rebellion. I simply didn't feel it was my calling." Telling her parents had been one of the hardest things she'd ever done and she still always felt as if she'd disappointed them. They didn't understand her desire to simply be a healer. In her parents' book, the only place to be was at the top of the food chain.

"I'll bet you always do what you're supposed to do, don't you, Shanahan? What's expected of you?"

If he'd been born into a family like hers, he would un-derstand that not everyone could just pack their stuff in a backpack and up and move to the middle of nowhere.

"You say it as if there's something wrong with living up to obligations. Why wouldn't I? That's what responsible people do."

"Don't you ever have the urge to do something you're not supposed to?" And there it was again, this tangle of sexuality between them, that drew her to him against her will, despite her knowing he was the wrong man for her.

*The urge to do something you're not supposed to do…*like kiss him? Like run her fingers through that thick unruly hair of his? "Not usually."

"I'm not so sure I believe that." She wasn't so sure she believed it when all she wanted to do was feel his lips on hers, know the tangle of his fingers in her hair and the press of his body against hers. "I've got some good news and some bad news for you."

"Okay."

"The bad news is I picked up an extra stop today on my run back from Sitka so I didn't have a chance to fix your shower." His voice took on a husky quality that did crazy things to her inside. "The good news is mine is still available."

She closed the lid on her empty take-out container. "I'll go get my things."

"Take your time. I get my shower first. Last night you ran me out of hot water. Trust me, I'm a whole helluva lot quicker than you. You want me to ring you when the shower's available?"

"Sure. That'll give me some time to get a few things done first." She opened the door and hesitated.

"Want me to walk you to your cabin?"

She almost accepted his offer but the sooner he finished his shower, the sooner she got hers. Plus, she needed a little distance from him to think things through.

"Thanks, it's a nice offer but I can manage."

"Careful, Shanahan. I think you just credited me with being nice." The banked fire in his eyes had her curling her hands inside her coat pocket. There was something about this man she couldn't resist.

"No worries, Saunders," she said, stopping on the threshold. "I'm sure you'll say or do something to dispel the notion sooner or later."

He was laughing as she closed the door behind her.

DALTON STRIPPED DOWN AND stepped into the shower, taking care to avoid wetting the bandage over his eye. He grabbed the bar of soap and lathered up.

There was no doubt in Dalton's mind that he and Skye were going to wind up in bed together. As Merrilee put it, the chemistry had been there from the beginning. Whether Skye knew it or not, she had some rebellion in her. He couldn't imagine what it must have taken to face her formidable family and announce she was breaking with tradition.

In all his wanderings, he'd never stumbled across a woman like her before and he suspected he never would again. And her? She'd go back home in a few weeks and her brother-in-law or a friend of a friend would set her up with a neurosurgeon or some other doctor sporting impressive credentials and they'd set about curing their corner of the world together. It was for damn certain the man she wound up with wouldn't be anything like him. Her family's collective ambitions made his ex-fiancée's look like child's play. But there was something between him and Skye Shanahan… And where better to indulge her inner rebellion, which he was so sure she possessed, than here in Alaska…with him?

What happened at Shadow Lake would stay at Shadow Lake.

He usually shaved in the mornings, but he made a quick pass with the razor now, using the mirror mounted on the shower wall. She had fair skin and the last thing he wanted to do was saddle her with whisker burn.

Turning off the water, he hastily dried off and headed into his bedroom. He looked his clothes over, hesitating. If he were heading out to a bar or a date, it'd be different. But he wanted to seduce the woman in his cabin. If she came back in and found him wearing a pair of khaki slacks and a polo shirt, she'd think he'd lost his mind. But sweat pants and a sweat shirt just didn't cut it either. He wound up pulling on a pair of blue jeans and his favorite Notre Dame sweatshirt.

Aftershave or no aftershave? Exasperated with himself, he crossed back to the bathroom and slapped some on.

What was his problem? He was dithering worse than any woman. Maybe the problem was she wasn't just *any* woman. This was Dr. Skye Shanahan…and he wanted her in the worst kind of way.

SKYE HESITATED IN FRONT OF the pegs that held her clothes. What to take to put on after her shower? How did you seduce a man like Dalton Saunders? Actually, seduction was an art she didn't have a whole lot of experience in. Okay, make that no experience.

For the first time in her life she wasn't living under her family's microscope. Even when she'd gone to college, she'd never left Atlanta. Plus, Emory was both her parents' and her brother's alma mater. She realized that going to the Alaskan wilds afforded her the first measure of real freedom in her life. Even when she'd gone to the Caribbean as a graduation present to herself, it had been a resort her parents frequented and the wait staff were all well acquainted with the Shanahans. Skye had never let her hair down because she'd never had the opportunity and she'd been too busy repressing that side of herself to even notice. So, no, she'd never seduced a man before. And it was about damn time.

From the moment she'd first seen Dalton, he'd turned her world upside down. She had thought the whole outdated, wild west concept of having to be claimed by a man to keep others at bay to be ludicrous, but there was no denying the secret thrill she'd felt when they'd stepped into that bar, and with just a tightening of his hand on her shoulder, he'd claimed her to be his own.

In the most rudimentary animal order, he'd been the alpha male and she his alpha female. And she'd liked it—both parts—the claiming and the belonging to him.

This was Good Riddance, Alaska, about as far-flung

from her world as she was ever going to get. He was a man with a checkered past who was destined to never cross her path again.

Perhaps there *was* a bit of a rebel inside her. If ever there was a chance to live outside her box, this was it. And all of that reasoning aside—she wanted him. Her body grew hot and tight and wet when she was around him. She wanted his bare heat around her, inside her. She wanted Dalton Saunders.

Now, how to go about getting him? All of her clothes were just as he'd described them, trim pantsuits. She did have a pair of silk pajamas but she didn't want to be that obvious. That left her with a pair of sweat pants, a T-shirt and a hoodie from Victoria's Secret that Bridgette had given her for Christmas last year. That'd have to do. And she had to admit that the blue hoodie and sweats matched her eyes and the T-shirt in a swirl of greens and blues did something for her skin and hair.

Then she snagged a push-up bra with matching panties and double-checked her toiletry case for the three-pack strip of condoms.

Ever since she'd been old enough to fully understand the importance of safe sex, she'd been a condom-carrying woman of the twenty-first century. Not that she'd ever had reason to use them in a situation like this but every year she threw out the old and replaced her supply with the new—no latex breakdown, thank you very much.

Now, she was fairly certain three condoms over the next two weeks wasn't going to be nearly enough. Great!

It wasn't as if she was an anonymous face in the check-out line at some corner drugstore back home. Nope, everyone in Good Riddance would know she was stocking up on prophylactics. The repressed Shanahan side of her felt a little horrified at the thought of her sex life being public knowledge. The Skye side of her merely smiled and shrugged. Wasn't that the whole scenario they'd set up at Gus's earlier tonight anyway? And actually, there was a part of her that was kind of proud of the fact that she was about to have a sex life again. It was a normal physical need. A natural part of life. What was unnatural, come to think of it, was how seldom that need had been met.

If she thought she could pull it off, she'd offer to kiss Saunders and make him feel better. But she'd just sound like an idiot saying it—she'd flush and blush and it would merely sound awkward.

Enough. Unless she was grossly mistaken, Saunders was moderately attracted to her. She'd quit trying to be something she wasn't. She'd just let things unfold as they would.

And if that didn't work, she'd simply jump his bones.

10

SKYE'S "PHONE" BUZZED and she jumped, her nerves getting the better of her.

"I'll meet you on your front porch," Saunders said.

"Okay." Her pulse began to race, but then again, he affected her that way. She'd enjoyed dates and relationships well enough, but no one had ever affected her like this. She finally got the meaning of the term "turned on." It was as if he literally flipped a switch and everything inside her was more tuned in, heightened, on standby just for him.

She drew a deep, steadying breath, slung her bag over her shoulder and headed out. He was just walking up the steps as she closed the door behind her.

"Ready?"

He had no idea. "Ready."

She welcomed the kiss of the cold night air against her flushed skin as they moved between cabins. She was heated from the inside out, and while the cool air didn't lessen her inner heat, she welcomed the contrast.

The moonlight illuminated his rakish grin. "I left you some hot water."

"Sorry about last night." This conversation sounded so intimate, as if they were already lovers. Or maybe she was just hyper tuned-in to everything.

He rested his fingers against the small of her back, guiding her along the path, and his touch seemed to burn through her clothes. Anticipation pooled between her thighs.

"Let's just say I was happy to skip a cold shower tonight."

Well, if she had anything to do with it—and she fully intended to—he wouldn't need any cold showers for the next several days.

He opened his cabin door and she preceded him into the warm room. A sudden onset of nerves attacked her. She was being ridiculous—she could keep a cool head under the most intense medical emergency, but let her think about seducing this man in his cabin and she fell apart. Nonetheless, she headed for the bathroom. She turned at the doorway, "I'm…um—" she pointed toward the bathroom "—just going to shower now."

"Do you maybe want a glass of wine after your shower?" he said, sounding almost as awkward as she did.

"That'd be nice." She closed the bathroom door and leaned against it, her knees a tad on the weak side. The room smelled like his aftershave and she closed her eyes, inhaling the scent, *his* scent. She liked it.

She made quick work of stripping out of her work

clothes and hopping under the warm spray of water. There was something faintly erotic and naughty about being naked in the same room he'd been naked in just a short time ago. She didn't linger, as she had last night, but she did take the time to shave her legs.

After smoothing lotion over her still-damp skin, she blow-dried her hair, dressed and touched up her make-up. She left her work clothes hanging on a hook on the back of the door and repacked her travel bag. Reaching for the door knob, she paused and whirled around for one final hair/clothes/makeup check. Maybe it was because she felt sexy when she was around Dalton, but Skye surprised herself with just how good she looked.

Sucking in a deep, steadying breath, she turned the knob and stepped out into the den.

"White wine, right?" he said, from the shadows of the kitchen across the room.

"Yes, white is perfect." A fire crackled in the fireplace and only the lamp at the end of the sofa was lit. Two glasses of wine waited on the coffee table.

"Feel better after your shower?" He crossed the room and sat down.

She took a seat on the couch, not quite knowing what to do with her body. Should she tuck one leg underneath her? Put both feet on the floor? Should she face straight ahead, or cant her body slightly toward his? She settled for shifting slightly in his direction and grabbing on to her wine glass as if it was a life preserver.

"Much better," she said with a laugh. "I can live without a lot of things, but showers are a necessity. Speaking of showers, what does your day look like tomorrow?"

"Very busy." His slow, deliberate smile sent a shiver through her. "I may be too busy to get that shower of yours repaired until after you leave."

He was flirting with her. She relaxed into the moment and smiled at him over the rim of her wine glass. "Is that a fact?"

The expression in his eyes was totally gratifying to her female ego. "If it means I get to see you in the evenings with your hair down like that, then yes, it is a fact."

He did seem to like her wild, crazy hair. And oddly enough, her wild crazy hair didn't seem nearly as out of place here, with him, as it always had when she was back at home. She twirled her finger around a curl and his eyes darkened. "There are other ways you could see me with my hair down in the evenings."

"Are there now?" His voice was low and soft.

She sipped at her wine. "Yes…you could ask."

He stretched his arm along the back of the sofa, his fingertips nearly touching her shoulder. "Ah, so that's what I've been doing wrong. Does asking always get a yes?"

She pretended to consider for a moment, "Not always, but often."

"Hmm, if asking only means often, I'd rather not fix your shower. That's a sure thing."

She laughed.

"Shanahan?" He caught some of her hair between his two fingers.

"Yes?"

"Do you think I could get another house call?" He twined her hair around his fingers and tugged, bringing her closer to him. "I think I'm in need of immediate medical attention."

"What seems to be the problem?"

"Dizziness, fever."

She ran her fingers over his forehead. "Hmm, you might be a little warm." She leaned in closer. "And maybe your pupils are a little dilated."

And then, they were kissing. Hungry, eager kisses. His hands were in her hair and his tongue explored the intimate recesses of her mouth. Somehow, in the tangle of mouths and hands, she was suddenly beneath him on the couch. She welcomed his weight, the hard press of his body against hers. He kissed and nipped along her neck and shoulder and she gave herself over to the glorious sensations rippling through her.

"It should be criminal for you to wear your hair any way other than this," he murmured against her ear.

"It's not very professional."

He leaned up on one elbow, the fire etching his features on one side, leaving the other in the shadow. "No, it's not. On second thought, you're absolutely right. You should only wear it this way at home because you're beautiful and sexy and I know what I think of when your hair is down like this. If all the other guys start thinking the same thing, someone will end up with more than a busted eye."

"That's positively Neanderthal, Saunders. And what exactly do you think about when my hair is down?"

He shifted and they were lying face-to-face on the couch, the sofa cushions against her back. "Doing this." He teased his tongue along the edge of her ear and she had a new appreciation for just how many nerve endings subsided there. "And this," he breathed against her neck, then scattered kisses while he traced the curve of her hip with his hand, cupping her buttock.

She slid her palm beneath the hem of his sweatshirt and her fingers encountered warm, muscled male flesh. "I never thought I'd hear myself say this, but I like the way you think."

"Stranger things have happened," he said. And then they were kissing again. Long, slow, drugging kisses that heightened her senses to nearly impossible levels and heated her body. He smelled good, tasted good, felt good. She moaned into his open mouth when he found her breasts with his hands.

Dalton shifted, so he was on the bottom and she was lying atop him. It was impossible to miss the hard ridge of his erection pressing against her. His penis definitely hadn't dropped off when she'd taken the wheel of his truck earlier in the evening.

"Will you be cold if you take off your jacket?" he asked, his voice low, husky, wanting.

She thought she could probably plunge into a snow drift and not be cold right now. "No. I'll be fine." He eased the hoodie over her shoulders and down her arms and tossed it to the floor. "Now you," she said.

She canted up enough so that he could peel his sweat-shirt up and over. Now they were T-shirt to T-shirt. He wrapped his arms around her and she lowered her head to kiss him. My God, the man could kiss. She sucked and nipped at his lower lip and he groaned. Her breasts felt heavy and ripe and her nipples welcomed the press against the wall of his chest.

"Hmm," he murmured as she rubbed herself against him. He trailed his hands down the curve of her back and slid them beneath the waist of her sweats, his palms sliding against her panties and over the rounded curve of her cheeks.

Sweet mercy.

"Do you want—"

"Yes."

He laughed softly, his fingers tightening against her buttocks. "But you don't even know what I was going to ask."

"Unless you're asking if I want to stop, the answer is yes."

DALTON FINALLY UNDERSTOOD THE appeal of slot ma-chines because he felt as if he'd just hit the jackpot. This incredible, sexy woman was about to be in his bed.

"Put your arms around my neck and wrap your legs around my waist," he said.

"My pleasure," she said, then skimmed her tongue

along the column of his throat. A shudder ran through him. Her touch was like some potent drug.

He carried her across the cabin and toed open the bedroom door. "It's cooler in here without the fireplace but there's so much more room."

"I think we'll heat it up in no time."

He laughed and she joined him. There was an exuberance about her that he hadn't anticipated. And then their mouths were fused back together and his hands explored curves and smooth skin while hers took the same journey over his body. She grasped the edge of his T-shirt and tugged it up. She uttered one word, "Off."

He pulled his shirt up and over his head and then helped divest her of her own. Blue jeans and sweat pants followed until they were skin on skin except for underwear. And the room was too damn dark. Moonlight came through the window but it wasn't enough. It wasn't nearly enough.

"Skye, I want to turn on the light."

"Why?"

"Because I want to see you in color. I've thought about your red hair spread out on my white pillowcase, your pale skin with those freckles, your gorgeous blue eyes."

"You have?"

"All damn day. All I could think about was you here, like this, or the way you're about to be."

"I hope you're not disappointed."

"Honey, the only way you could possibly disappoint

me would be if you got up and walked out of that door."

He reached over and flipped on the bedside lamp. He tugged down the cover on one side of the bed, then laying her down, he leaned back and looked his fill. Black lace panties and a black bra provided stark contrast to her white skin. Her belly and breasts were like fine porcelain. Freckles kissed her arms, legs and shoulders. It was easy to see where the sun had never touched. "You take my breath away, Skye Shanahan."

Her mouth blossomed into a slow, sweet smile. "I could say the same, Dalton Saunders."

He eased down next to her and she rolled readily to him, sliding her leg in between his, strumming her fingers over his belly and up his chest. Part of him wanted to rip her bra and panties off and simply take her into oblivion but another part of him wanted to savor her. Ripping her clothes off would be another day, another time. Tonight called for relishing each morsel of her that was revealed.

He kissed her neck, the hollow of her throat, the indention formed by the small nest of bones above her breasts. He heard her intake of breath as he skimmed the rounded mound spilling over the top of her black lace bra. He reached up and pulled her straps off her shoulders and then he bent his head and tugged one of the cups down with his teeth, then the other, until both of her breasts spilled over the bra's top. "Perfection, Shanahan, perfection."

Deep-pink hued nipples stood outlined against her

milky white globes. He swirled his tongue around the turgid peak and she buckled up off the bed. He gave the other one the same attention and she fisted her hands in the sheets.

He lapped at her sweet tip and then took the entire thing in his mouth and sucked. Her hands gripped his head and she panted, "Yes, that feels so good, yes."

He divided his attention evenly until he couldn't stand it any longer and he slid down her body, kissing a trail over her flat belly. He skimmed her panties down over the side of her hips, down the length of her legs. A neatly trimmed thatch of bright red springy curls covered the juncture of her thighs.

"You are so beautiful," he said, needing to kiss her, wanting to touch her. His lips found hers at the same time his finger delved into her wet curls. Her cry echoed inside their kiss and he matched it with his own groan. She wrapped her tongue around his, sucking on it and he felt as if he might very well explode.

She was ready and he was for damn sure past ready.

"Honey—" he said, his breath ragged.

"Yes."

He opened the condom and rolled it on. Grasping her legs between his hands, he positioned himself between her thighs.

And that's when she screamed bloody murder.

_11_

FOR A SECOND SHE COULDN'T speak, as if that scream had used up all the air in her lungs. Then she found her voice again.

"Someone at the window." Skye sucked in a ragged breath. "There was someone at the bedroom window."

Saunders swore and jumped off the bed.

"Where are you going?" she said, even though she knew. But the very idea panicked her.

He skipped his underwear and pulled on his jeans. "To make sure whoever it was is gone."

That was what she feared. "What if they're not? What if they're armed?"

His mouth was grim, his eyes hard. "They'll be one sorry son of a bitch, that's what."

As long as he was in the cabin, he was safe. Once he walked out that door, all bets were off. "You can't leave me in here alone."

He'd pulled on his sweatshirt and stepped into his boots. He headed for the den and she scrambled off the bed, snatching up her sweatpants and T-shirt. "Lock the door behind me and I'll leave you a gun."

He jerked on his winter coat hanging on a peg by the front door.

"I don't know how to shoot a gun," she said as she hopped on one foot and then the other into her sweats, then tugged her T-shirt on.

"You're smart. You'll figure it out," he said, pulling a handgun out of cabinet beneath his gun rack and handing it to her.

The gun felt heavy and foreign in her hand. "Maybe I should come with you."

"Stay in here. Don't unlock this door until you hear me on the other side." He pulled her to him and kissed her quick and hard. "And for God's sake, don't shoot me."

Grabbing a rifle off the gun rack, he snatched up a flashlight and stalked out the door. "Lock it, Skye."

She did as he'd instructed and tried to gather her wits. If asked for a description, she'd be hard-pressed to give any information other than the man had a beard, that much she was sure of, and he'd been wearing a cap. And he'd been peering through the window.

She forced herself to examine the gun Dalton had thrust into her hands. If she was called upon to defend Dalton or herself, it'd be inexcusable if she was incapable. He'd told her she was smart and she was. Surely she could figure out something with which the most base, uneducated criminal was proficient. And studying the gun took her mind off of whether her would-be lover was safe or whether he'd been overtaken.

She was practicing taking aim down what appeared to be a sight on the barrel when she heard someone coming up the stairs. "It's me, Skye. Open the door."

"How can I be sure it's you?"

"You puked in my plane yesterday."

She threw the latch and he came in, stomping snow off his boots at the door's threshold, snow dusting his dark hair. "He's gone." She nearly sagged with relief. Instead, she took the flashlight from him and returned it to the hook by the door. She also put the gun he'd handed her back on top of the chest as he stepped out of his boots.

"I heard the truck. There's a light snow outside so it was easy to track his footprints. He'd circled around your cabin and then obviously saw the light in my bedroom." Dalton re-racked his shotgun and shrugged out of his jacket. "He'd left a truck out on the road. There were tire tracks coming in and tire tracks going out."

"Oh, God." Now that she knew they were safe, reality set in. She felt violated. Someone had stood at Dalton's bedroom window and seen them, watched them. She began to shake uncontrollably.

Strong, warm arms enfolded her, supported her, cradling her close to his chest. She burrowed into Dalton's warmth, his solidness. His big hands stroked her back, "Shh. Shh. Shh. It's okay. It's going to be fine. You were magnificent. And you're going to stay here tonight." His voice subtly shifted from soothing to commanding.

"I'm sure whoever it was isn't coming back tonight, but there's no way in hell you're going to be in that cabin next door alone." He wouldn't get any argument from her on that. She wouldn't sleep a wink if she had to stay by herself tonight. "It's fine, honey. Really it is."

They were safe and she'd be here with him. Given that load off her mind, her brain backed up to something he'd said previously. She leaned back in his arms and looked up at him—the strong column of his throat, the resolute line of his jaw, the honesty in his eyes. "Magnificent? I was magnificent?"

His lips curled in that smile of his that always left her feeling warm and mixed up inside. "Do you know how many women would've fallen apart? Been hysterical?"

"But I was almost hysterical now," she said, feeling compelled to confess her weakness.

He smoothed her hair back from her face, his touch tender. "This isn't horseshoes, Shanahan. Almost doesn't count. When it mattered, you came through."

"You think so?" Saunders really had no idea just how damn scared she'd been for him. Actually, until he'd walked back through that door, she wasn't sure she'd realized just how frightened she'd been.

"I know so," he said.

A drop of water slid down his cheek. The snow in his hair was melting. "Hold on a second," she said, sprinting to the bathroom. She grabbed a towel and hurried back. "Here, let me…" she said, as she reached up and towel-dried his damp hair and face, blotting carefully around the bandage over his eye.

He caught her hand and brought her fingers to his mouth, pressing a kiss to them. "Thanks, Doc."

There was a tenderness, a sweetness to the gesture that arrowed straight through her. She'd never wanted a man more than she wanted Dalton Saunders, bad choice and all.

SHE LOOKED SLIGHTLY stunned and he supposed that while he was used to the craziness that sometimes made up Alaska, this was a rude exposure to the sometimes wild and woolly north.

"Are you okay?" he said.

She shook her head slightly, as if to clear it and smiled. "Hey, that's my line—you're the patient." She lightly touched the area above his bandage and he thought once again that a woman's touch had never stirred him the way hers did, doctor or not. "That okay?"

"Fine." He clenched his hand. "The son of a bitch is lucky I didn't catch up with him."

"I wouldn't want him to cross my path right now, either. Forget that he saw me naked, but he interrupted us on the verge of what was probably going to be the best sex I've ever had."

They'd definitely broken the mold with Skye Shanahan. "The best sex ever? Really?"

"Forget I said that."

"Like hell I will. And that was exactly why I would've

shot the son of a bitch. I've wanted you from the first moment I set eyes on you."

"You have?" Her brilliant blue eyes widened.

"Admit it, Shanahan. You wanted me, too." They'd struck sparks from the beginning.

A slyness colored her smile. "Maybe." She laughed at his expression. "Okay. Yes. I wanted you, too."

If she was coming clean, so was he. What the hell, why hold back? He buried his head in the soft cloud of her hair. "Last night, I thought I would lose my mind lying in my bed, wondering what you were…or weren't wearing."

"Silk pajamas." She smiled impishly and he had a glimpse of what she must've been like as a little girl, before she was weighed down with family expectation. He knew, without a doubt, that family expectation played a major factor in Dr. Skye Shanahan's life. "I don't actually own anything flannel."

Joy of simply having her here in his arms, in his life, teasing him, spilled out of him in laughter.

"Silk. I'll have to remember that for future fantasies. But today, when I fantasized about you in my bed, you were naked."

A faint blush tinged her pale skin but the expression in her eyes said she liked it. He went for broke. "And then, when you were actually there, you were even better than my fantasy. So, when that sonofabitch intruded… Hell yeah, I would've shot him."

"I'm sorry, Saunders, but I can't sleep…or anything

else in your bedroom. I think I'll have nightmares about that window."

"Are you okay with this room if I cover the windows?"

"Yes. But how are we both going to fit on the couch?"

"We're not." He quickly shoved the couch and coffee table over closer to the front door. Grinning, he grabbed her hand and tugged her toward the bedroom, "Come on. Work with me here. We'll bring the mattress in and set it up in front of the fireplace. How does that suit you, Doc?"

"You'd move your mattress for me?"

"Of course." Hell, he'd probably try to move a mountain for her if it would put that expression on her face again. "You grab the blankets and pillows and I'll bring the mattress."

"Deal."

Within minutes he'd draped towels over the windows and had the mattress set up in the den. He threw another couple of logs on the fire, stoking it to burn well into the night.

She linked her arms around his waist and nuzzled at his neck. "I was thinking, Saunders... We can't let that guy win by ruining the evening, so I vote we take up where we left off." She reached beneath his sweatshirt. "Well, maybe we need to rewind just a little bit to get things back to where they were when Tom showed up."

"Tom?" Had she recognized the guy after all?

"Peeping Tom."

"I am all for rewinding."

IT WAS QUITE POSSIBLY the most romantic set-up she'd ever seen, perhaps in part because Dalton had been willing to do all of this for her. And maybe there was a smidgen of pioneer spirit in her, because while the whole incident had been somewhat terrifying, it had also been exhilarating. Good grief, when Saunders had pulled her in for that quick, hard kiss before going out to defend the cabin, well, there was a reason they wrote those kind of moments into scripts and novels. It was the stuff heroes were made of. It was the stuff that, in retrospect, made a woman almost swoon even if she wasn't the swooning type. And Skye was pretty proud of herself, too, for figuring out the gun. It didn't hurt that Saunders had applauded her as "magnificent."

Saunders sat on the mattress edge and took her hands in his. "So, now, where were we just before we were so rudely interrupted?" A gentle tug on his part brought her down to the mattress with him.

"Well, for starters, we both were wearing a lot less clothes."

"Well, by all means, Shanahan, let me give you a hand with that. I like you best naked."

She wasn't sure whether she was flattered or offended. "What does that mean exactly?"

"It means that I'm a man and you're a beautiful woman with a great body. And just know that tomorrow, when you walk into your office looking all professional in your work clothes, I'm going to be seeing you like this."

Well. No man had ever said anything like that to her before and she found that she quite liked it. While the rest of the world saw her as their doctor, he would see the woman beneath. She found it intimate, exciting... arousing. "Hm. I think I like that."

Within a minute they were both naked on the mattress. She glanced at the fire. "This is nice." Emboldened by his forthright admiration, she reached between them and stroked him. "And this is even nicer."

He grinned and rolled her to her back. "Shanahan, I take back everything I thought about your lack of bedside manner."

She propped up on one elbow and pretended outrage. "Lack of bedside manner?"

"Don't worry. You can make it up to me now." He slipped his hands along her ribcage and his touch whispered heat across her skin.

"So, exactly what do you consider an appropriate bedside manner, Saunders?" She sucked in a deep breath as he plied his thumbs along the underside of her breasts.

"Well, I think it needs to vary case by case. Bring home your lab coat tomorrow and we could figure it out."

She leaned into him and nuzzled at his jaw, inhaling the scent of him, as he moved his hands higher on her breast. "Is this some kind of latent, unfulfilled playing doctor fantasy?"

"I never knew I had one before but I seem to have developed one now." His fingers found her nipples and the sensation arrowed straight to her core.

Skye moaned deep in her throat and pushed her breasts harder into his hands. "That sounds serious. I'll try to remember to bring my coat home tomorrow." She would *so* be bringing that white coat home with her.

"I'll remind you," he said.

She found his male nipple with her tongue and flicked the edge of it. His breath hissed against her bare skin. He was a delicious mix of satin skin, muscle and just the right amount of chest hair that arrowed down to his belly and past that to his groin. He was, in her estimation, male perfection.

She slid her hand down his belly and thigh to boldly stroke the length of his penis. Ah. She curved her fingers around him. He was hot and hard and she wanted him inside her.

"Speaking of reminding, I think this is where we left off before."

"Hmm. I think you're right." He rolled on another condom and her body was tight and slick with anticipation of what was to come, of the feel of him inside her.

Without any self-consciousness, she spread her legs, inviting him where she wanted him most. He paused, his eyes glittering, his face tight, his voice husky. "You are beautiful."

"So are you," she said. And he was. Backlit by the fire, washed in shadows, he was rugged, lean and fit with an edge of the untamed in his dark, slightly long hair and bandaged eye.

He leaned forward, his mouth capturing hers in a kiss. She wrapped her hands around his neck, winnowing her hands into his dark hair, pulling him closer, tighter, harder into her. For the first time ever, she felt truly free to be who and what she wanted. She ached with a need, a want more intense than anything she'd ever experienced before.

Dalton eased into her and she gasped into his mouth. Yes. And then he withdrew, shifting a little deeper on the next entry. Her body welcomed him, rose to meet his thrusts.

She lost herself in the taste of his tongue and lips, the feel of his chest against her breasts, the fullness of him inside her. Even as the physical element built inside her, winding her tighter and tighter, emotionally she fell harder and deeper. It wasn't just a melding of bodies, she gave of her spirit, of herself with each thrust, each kiss.

Dalton buried himself inside her and instead of thrusting he began a slow, deliberate grind against her. She felt the first ripples of her orgasm begin and she gave herself over to it completely. She cried out as she soared higher and higher, finally shattering in satisfaction.

12

DALTON PULLED UP IN FRONT of the Skye's office. It had been strange to wake up with her in his bed this morning. It had been a long time since he'd shared a bathroom and the morning ritual of getting ready for work with a woman. For all that there had been the awkward moment or two, she was amazingly easy to be around. She'd just sort of gone about her business while he went about his.

She reached for the door handle and he stopped her. "You need to let Nelson know what happened last night. I don't want to frighten you, but I'd say it's likely that whoever visited you last night is going to show up at some point today." Dammit to hell, it made him angry all over again to think of someone trespassing and scaring her that way. Not to mention, seeing her naked. "Make sure Nelson knows so he has your back."

She nodded, a faint shadow of apprehension flitting across her face. "I'll apprise Nelson. Fly safe today."

"Thanks." He didn't want her day to start out on a

sour note, so he added, "Hey, Doc, don't forget that lab coat this evening." He looked across the expanse of the truck's cab and in his head, her hair was already tumbling down about her shoulders and she was wearing nothing but her underwear and that white coat. And much like going full-throttle on an ascent, that had quite the effect on his body.

A blush crawled up her fair skin. "You're doing it, aren't you?" She moistened her lower lip with the tip of her tongue and he knew she knew precisely what he was thinking and it was equally arousing for her.

"Uh-huh. And don't forget your breakfast." He handed off her portion of their brown-bagged breakfast. They'd swung by Gus's and picked up fresh, hot cinnamon rolls. She had enough for her and Nelson, whom she deemed a lifesaver. If Skye hadn't wound up in Dalton's bed last night, he might've felt a twinge or a little more than a twinge of jealousy over Nelson, but she had so he didn't. "Got to keep up your strength."

"You're incorrigible, Saunders." Her smile said she fully appreciated it, however.

"I know, Shanahan. And if any of your male patients look at you like that today, call me so I can come kick their ass."

She laughed as she climbed out of his truck. "Bye, Saunders."

"See ya, Shanahan."

He watched her until she disappeared through the door, liking that she knew that he was watching. He drove over to the airstrip and grabbed his own breakfast as he headed in, whistling beneath his breath. He hadn't felt this good in…well, maybe forever.

Merrilee was sitting at the desk, filling out a report when he walked in. "Morning, Merrilee." The aroma of strong, fresh-brewed coffee scented the air. Most mornings Jeb Taylor and Dwight Simmons were waiting on Merrilee to open so they could take up residence by the pot-bellied stove. But on Tuesday mornings when Gus turned out her cinnamon rolls, the two men spent the first half of their day holed up at her place.

Merrilee took one look at him and nodded. "I see."

Dalton hung his coat by the door. "You see what?"

She tapped her cheek with the eraser-end of her pencil, a knowing smile on her face. "I see how things went last night."

"I'll tell you what happened last night," he said, pouring a steaming mug of joe.

Merrilee held up a staying hand. "I don't need details."

"Don't worry." He sat in the chair next to her desk, stretching out his legs and reaching for his breakfast. "You won't get any of those details from me. But I thought you'd want to know that someone came out and was snooping around the cabins. Skye saw him looking through the window."

Merrilee's smile faded and a frown creased her forehead. "That must've scared the poor girl half to death. She's going to think we're all crazy as coots."

"I believe she does." He bit into the warm dough,

cinnamon and sugar melting against his tongue. Damn, Gus could outcook anyone, anywhere.

"Any idea who it was?" Merrilee stood and topped off her coffee cup, visibly agitated. For all that she possessed a backbone of steel—and she had to have had one to have founded a town and made it here—there was an element of idealism about her. The fight at Gus's place last night wouldn't have fazed her, but the idea of someone peering in windows at someone else, particularly a visitor, didn't sit well with her.

"No idea who it was. Could've been anybody. She said he had a cap and a beard."

She pursed her lips. "That just described ninety percent of Alaska's male population."

Dalton polished off the last of the cinnamon roll and washed it down with the strong brew. "Exactly. And whoever it was won't come back if they know what's good for them."

"Thank goodness those cabins have that call system," Merrilee said, obviously fishing, leveling her gaze on him.

What was the point in beating around the bush? "She wasn't in her cabin, she was in mine. I'm going to move her in with me for the rest of the time she's here. Besides, I don't think she cared for Irene's trophy display." They might not get much sleep, at least they hadn't last night, but it wouldn't be because he was worried about somebody looking in her window. Or because he was wondering just what she was, or wasn't, wearing when she was snuggled in her bed next door.

She'd worn his skin against hers last night and that had suited him just fine.

Reaching for the clipboard with the day's flight schedule printed out, Merrilee said, "I only see one thing wrong with that plan."

"Yeah, what's that?"

She passed him his copy. "You might get used to her being there."

He was used to living alone. He didn't foresee it being a problem when it was time for her to head back to the lower forty-eight. "Nearly two weeks of playing house should be just about right. She'll be ready to go and I'll be ready for her to go."

This time there was a serious note in her voice. "And what if you're not?"

What the heck? She was worried about *him?* "Merrilee, I don't want to have to dive for cover or anything, but I barely escaped a committed relationship when I left my mind-numbing job eight years ago. Day-by-day is my motto. And two weeks will be plenty."

"Famous last words."

Merrilee always had to have a say and he let her this time, but he knew what he knew. He wanted Skye Shanahan and she wanted him. But they were worlds apart and they both knew it was strictly temporary.

"THANKS FOR THE CINNAMON rolls," Nelson said, offering his steady smile.

"You're welcome. Thanks for the coffee."

"I'll keep an eye open today. If anything strikes you as wrong, don't worry about making a scene. Yell."

Over coffee and pastries, Skye had filled Nelson in on all the facts, only leaving out that she'd been naked in Dalton's bed, since that didn't seem particularly pertinent. "So you think whoever it was will show up today, too?" That had been Dalton's theory.

"I'd say it's likely."

Skye got up from behind her desk and washed her hands in the corner sink, mostly for something to do with her nervous energy. "I think it's going to be a long day."

Nelson shot her a sympathetic glance, "We're going to be so busy today, time will fly by. And now I'd better go unlock the front door."

Several hours later, Nelson had proved to be right. She'd lanced a boil, told a young bride she was about to be a new mommy, wrapped a sprained wrist, diagnosed a gall bladder attack and set up a surgical consult in Anchorage for the patient, just to name a few things. For the most part, everyone was incredibly nice. But each appointment took extra time because every patient wanted a chance to spend a few personal minutes with the visiting doctor and find out about her life back in the "lower forty-eight."

Ducking into her office, Skye pulled the door closed behind her. She perched on the edge of the desk—those flowers on the wall were beginning to grow on her a little—and unwrapped the pimento cheese sandwich Gus had sent over.

While she ate, she allowed herself the luxury of thinking about Dalton. Making love in front of the fire had been incredible. Even now, in the middle of her day with those flowers staring back at her from the wall, a hot need blossomed inside her. He was a thoughtful, considerate lover and there were parts of her that were aching today because they hadn't been used in quite some time.

She popped the last bite into her mouth and stood. Sitting around thinking about Dalton wouldn't get her patients seen. And the sooner her patients were taken care of, the sooner she'd be back at Shadow Lake with him.

Shutting Dalton out of her mind, she picked up the chart outside the exam-room door and quickly scanned Nelson's notes. Normal vitals. Possible gastrointestinal problem.

A professional smile on her face, Skye entered the exam room. The moment she walked in, she knew. The man on the exam table was the same man who'd peered through the window last night. She couldn't identify him, per se, but she recognized the way he looked at her.

He didn't leer, but recognition gleamed in his eyes. It took every ounce of her professionalism to continue forward and treat him the way any doctor would.

"Good afternoon, Mr. Culpepper. I'm Dr. Shanahan. What seems to be the problem today?"

He glanced down at the floor and mumbled, "Got sort of a burning in my gut."

"I see. Excuse me a moment, please. I'll be right back."

She was honor-bound by the Hippocratic oath to treat a person with a problem, but she didn't have to be alone with a man who'd violated her privacy. Nelson was across the hall in the chart room, which doubled as the lab and supply room.

"Nelson, would you step into the exam room, please?" she said, striving for a normal tone.

Nelson nodded, his dark eyes aware, his voice low. "It's Culpepper, isn't it?"

She worried her lower lip between her teeth and nodded. "I'm pretty sure." She wasn't quite whispering but she also spoke in an undertone. "How did you know?"

"He seemed nervous and I can see it in your face."

She straightened her spine and decided there was no shame in saying it. "I don't want to be in the exam room alone with him."

"No problem. I almost came in anyway."

Nelson followed her into the examination room and Skye launched into her spiel. "Okay, Mr. Culpepper, let's see if we can figure out what's wrong."

"Why's he in here?" he asked, jerking his head toward Nelson.

She was doubly glad she'd asked Nelson to come in. "He's here to observe. We train as we go."

The man's face crumpled. "You know, don't you? You know it was me?"

Nelson didn't attempt to act subtle as he placed

himself between her and Culpepper. Skye nodded an affirmative.

"I didn't mean no harm, Doc. Really, I didn't. I'd heard you and Dalton was together but I didn't believe it. I just wanted to knock on your door and meet you but you weren't home, so I did a little scouting. I promise you I'd just looked in when you looked up. I've been mighty lonesome since my wife up and left months ago."

She *almost* felt sorry for him. "You do understand that stalking someone isn't the best way to get off to a good start?"

Hanging his head, he mumbled, "I know that." He looked back up. "And I…uh…I was only at the window a second or two. But I saw, well, I reckon I don't much stand a chance now, do I?"

It took her a second to process that he really, sincerely was asking if he might have a chance with her. There was no way to let him down gently. And considering he seemed contrite enough and maybe he really had only just glanced in the window, she was blunt. "No, Mr. Culpepper, you don't."

He looked from her to Nelson. "You gonna mention it to Dalton?" Perspiration coated his face and there was no mistaking the apprehension in his eyes.

"I have to. It was his property."

"And you're his woman." His tone was nothing short of mournful.

"I'm not his property, Mr. Culpepper." These people really were in the Dark Ages. "The cabins are his property and he has a right to know."

He hopped off the table, apparently fear proving to be a miracle cure for his gastric distress. "Guess I'd better be heading back home then." He tugged on a billed cap. "Let him know I'll be bringing him a moose."

"You're bringing him a moose?"

Nelson, who'd been quiet up until then, spoke up. "Restitution."

He and Culpepper nodded at one another. Culpepper tweaked the bill of his cap in Skye's direction. "Apologies again, ma'am. You sure are a looker, though. Dressed and undressed."

That did it. That pushed her right over the edge. She spoke through gritted teeth. "Go. Out."

Culpepper shuffled out of the room and she turned to Nelson. Certainly not the first time since she'd been in Alaska, she felt on the verge of hysterical laughter. "I'm sure this is totally unnecessary for me to say, but if you breathe that last bit to anyone, I'll have to kill you. I know how to handle a gun now." This wild and woolly west fever must be catching.

He wisely managed not to laugh, but his eyes were dancing. "My lips are sealed, Dr. Skye."

"And just for the sake of elucidation, Culpepper's bringing Saunders a moose for trespassing on his property?"

"And looking at his woman in a state of undress."

Skye buried her face in her hands. She looked back up. "Dead or alive?"

"Dead. It's difficult to handle a live moose."

"It's not outside the realm of possibility in this place that he might have a pet moose."

"No. The moose will be dead. Dressed out."

"Dressed out?" Was that like the moose at Irene's cabin? Was that considered dressed out?

"Butchered. Cut and packaged for food."

"Oh. I see."

And she did indeed see. She was beginning to think like these people. And it scared the life out of her.

13

THAT EVENING ON THE WAY to Shadow Lake, Dalton kept one eye on the road and the other on Skye's face as she recounted her encounter with Culpepper. "So, I should expect a moose, eh?"

He turned into the driveway, angling her side closest to the cabin steps.

She wrinkled her nose. "That's what he said. Nelson explained it was restitution."

He threw the truck in Park and they both got out. "Culpepper can leave it with Gus." Every time he thought about Skye's scream and the look on her face, he wanted to throw a punch. And the son of a bitch had seen her naked. "If he ever sets foot on my property again, he'll be damned sorry. He didn't say anything off color to you, did he?" He opened the cabin door for her.

"Dalton, I'm perfectly capable of handling my own affairs."

"That sounds like a *yes* to me." He'd laid in a fire

before they left this morning and he squatted to start it now. He kept the heat on all day, but the fire would knock the chill off the room. "Hey, will you turn on the lamp?"

Dalton had lived alone for a long time. Not only was he used to it, he liked it. When he and Laura had been engaged, they'd lived together. When they'd broken up and he'd packed up and moved to Alaska, it had been something of a relief to have Laura out of his space. He'd certainly known Laura much longer and more intimately than he knew Skye, so you'd think it would feel awkward to have her in his cabin. But it wasn't, oddly enough. It felt natural, as if she belonged there. He hadn't thought twice about asking her to turn on the lamp.

"Sure." She clicked the knob and a soft glow lit that corner of the room. "I wasn't saying yes when I said I'd handle my own affairs. What I meant was *don't worry about it.*"

He realized he knew her well enough that the topic was now closed as far as she was concerned. "You're not going to tell me what he said, are you?"

"It's not important," she said, hanging her coat on the hook by the door. She turned to him with a smile that sent his temperature soaring exponentially. "I'll tell you what's important."

Raising his eyebrows in silent query at the promising expression on her face, he skirted the edge of the mattress in front of the hearth and spanned the area separating them. With a smile, she reached into her purse and pulled out a white folded square of cloth. "Lab coat." She shook it out.

"You remembered," he said.

"You forgot."

"Not exactly forgot. I was distracted by Culpepper." He ran his hands over her arms. "But now I'm about to be distracted by my favorite doctor making a house call." He found the pins holding her hair in its smooth twist. "May I?" He nuzzled the tender side of her neck. He loved the way she smelled. "I've wanted to do this for a very long time."

She laughed, stroking her fingers along his jaw. "You haven't known me for a very long time."

"Well, I've wanted to do it for as long as I've known you."

She scraped the tip of her fingernail along his neck and his body hummed. "Then do it," she whispered in his ear, her breath a warm, tantalizing touch against him. It was as if Skye reached deep inside him to that part of him that was raw and unguarded. It was both scary as hell and exhilarating.

He wanted her hair down, but he also wanted the rest. He dropped his hand to his side. "Wait. Go in the bathroom and come back out wearing just your underwear and your lab coat. That would make me very, very happy."

"Hmm. I want you very, very happy because I'm pretty sure that would translate into me being very happy."

He pulled her to him, letting his hard-on nestle

between her legs and kissed her, telling her without words just how much he wanted her and how sure he'd be to please her. Both of their breathing was unsteady when they broke apart.

"Hold that thought." She stepped out of his arms and he already missed her being there, but anticipation had him ramped up to an incredible level. "I'll be right back." He watched her cross the room, enjoying the view of her trim hips and cute little tush. She stopped at the bathroom door. With a cat-spotting-the-cream smile, she reached into her bag and tossed something across the room to him. "Open down the front." She closed the door behind her.

In about a split second after she closed the door, he realized he was holding a patient exam gown. He grinned all over himself. She was full of surprises.

"You lifted a gown from the clinic, Shanahan?" he called out as he stripped down. It was damn chilly in the room but they'd take care of that soon enough.

"It's not as if I stole it. I'll take it back." He could hear the laughter in her voice. Naked, he wrapped the thin cotton around him, tying it in the front. "And make sure your socks are off, too. That is so not sexy," she called out.

He looked down. Damn, how'd she know? In his haste to get ready, he'd forgotten his socks. He jumped on one foot as he tugged first one off and then the other, tossing them to the side.

"I'm ready," he yelled.

"Are you lying down?"

He dropped to his back, stretching out on the mattress. "I am now."

His heart was pounding like a runaway train when the creaking hinge heralded the bathroom door opening. "Oh. God." He didn't even realize he'd spoken aloud until she smiled a very sexy smile of acknowledgment.

She was everything—and so much more—than he'd ever imagined. Hair up, black-rimmed glasses on, lab coat, two-inch heels and all that gorgeous white skin with just a pair of high-on-the-thigh panties trimmed in lace and a matching plunge push-up bra. If he died right now, he'd go as a happy man. But if death was on the agenda, he'd prefer to wait about an hour, because then he'd die an ecstatic man. His dick quivered, bobbing like a pole out of control against the patient gown which was now tented over the lower half of his body.

She stopped at the edge of the mattress, and looked down at him, her blue eyes gleaming behind the lenses of her glasses. "Oh, I see right away that you have quite a problem, Mr. Saunders. But I'm still going to need to examine you."

She reached behind her head, her hand poised on the pin holding her hair up. "Me or you?"

Admittedly it would be hot to see her take her hair down, but tonight, he wanted to do it. "Me."

She leaned down as he reached up. The lamp's glow and the fire's flame lent her skin a porcelain cast, but she was all soft, warm woman. He released her hair and it tumbled around her face and shoulders in a cascade of red fire. Heat roared through him. He'd never seen anything sexier in his life.

She leaned farther over and her hair tickled his skin. He gritted his teeth. There was nothing for it but to say it. "I wanted this game, but we're going to have to play fast because…I'm too strung out. I don't think I'm going to last very long."

"I know exactly what you mean." Her eyes and the tautness of her features said she was in the same boat he was. "But I've got to examine you to determine your problem."

She untied the front of the gown and spread it open, leaving him naked. Her smile was that of a temptress as she said, "Tell me if it hurts."

And then her hands and mouth were moving over him, stroking, licking, kneading, kissing his neck, his chest, his belly, his hip while her hair danced across those same areas. It was a heady, intoxicating mix of pleasure almost bordering on pain. It felt so damn good. He would swear his dick had never been this hard, this throbbing. He felt as if he might damn well explode.

She uttered a small laugh and said, "I think I've found your problem." She didn't touch his cock but her mouth was so close, he could feel the warmth of her breath against his erection. She moved her head slightly and a swath of her hair brushed over him. It was like an electric shock jolting through him. He groaned, clenching his belly muscles to keep from coming then and there.

"We've definitely located the source of your discomfort." Her words might have sounded professional but her breathing held a ragged edge.

He couldn't speak. He was using every ounce of his self-control to hold himself in check. She ran her fingers up his shaft in a gossamer light touch and he inhaled a deep breath and closed his eyes.

"I'd say you're definitely running a fever."

And then her tongue was on him and around him and his entire body shuddered when she took him in her wet, warm mouth. He fisted his hand in her hair and stopped her. She released him.

"There's only one treatment for what you have," she said, straddling him. She slid her wet panties along his throbbing cock. She threw her head back and closed her eyes and he knew she wanted him inside her as desperately as he wanted to be there. She reached into her lab coat and silently pulled out a condom. There was so much tension, so much excitement, so much need pulsing between them, around them, through them, words weren't necessary.

He took the condom, ripped open the wrapper and rolled it on. She braced her hands on his shoulders. He tugged her panties to one side. Even as she came down, he surged up and a guttural sound tore from his throat at the feel of her surging down on him, taking him all the way inside her hot, wet channel.

It was a hard, fast ride and her short, sharp moans told him she was coming as quickly as he was. She clenched and convulsed around him as he found his own release with another guttural shout.

"Hmm. I think you're cured," she said as she collapsed against his chest, with him still deep inside her.

He smiled against her hair but he wasn't so sure. He doubted there'd ever be a cure for her.

"DID YOU EVER CONSIDER being a commercial airline pilot?" The second the question left her mouth she regretted it. There was no way he could fly commercially if he was a convicted felon.

She loved that sated look in his eyes.

"The big birds aren't the same. I wasn't ever interested in that."

But she was still stuck on the other point and maybe it was tacky to bring it up, but it was like the elephant in the room. She had to mention it. "How'd you get a pilot's license with a prison record?"

He leaned up on one elbow and reached over with the other hand to play with her hair. He definitely had a fixation with her hair and that definitely suited her just fine. "I've never been in prison. You jumped to that conclusion. It's what you wanted to think, so I let you."

She jacked up into a sitting position, dragging the sheet up along with her. What? "But, I...you said..."

"You're disappointed? You really were in full rebel mode, weren't you?"

"No, I'm not disappointed, thank you very much. I'm actually relieved." She narrowed her eyes in accusation. "You led me to believe you were a felon." She wasn't exactly angry, more disconcerted. This just brought home to her that she'd just been extremely intimate with a man that she knew very little about and the bits she thought she knew were erroneous.

The rise and fall of his broad shoulders was totally unrepentant. "I mentioned a 'fresh start' and you made the quantum leap to 'I'd done time.'"

She squirmed a little against the mattress. "Maybe I did arrive with a few prejudices." And maybe she had wanted to paint him as inappropriate, as off-limits as possible.

"You think?"

Reaching over, Skye playfully punched his arm, "Hey, you still were misleading."

"I had done time." His expression grew serious. "I was doing corporate time—the daily grind of a commute, a suit and tie and office politics."

He was totally upending her concept of him. "What kind of job?"

"Accounting. CPA." He named a Big Ten firm she recognized immediately.

Accounting? He'd been a CPA? She sat there for a minute, narrowing her eyes, trying to reconcile the free-spirited, rugged bush pilot in front of her with a yuppy bean counter. She could mentally cut his hair and deck him out in a staid Brooks Brothers ensemble but she simply couldn't box his energy and irreverence and put it behind a desk. She didn't have that much imagination. "And you just woke up one morning and walked away?"

"Something like that."

"You just threw it all away? The college, the job, everything?" She was conflicted. Part of her was horrified at the total irresponsibility of it. But there was another part of her, perhaps a part that she was just beginning to recognize and acknowledge, that applauded the sheer bravado of such a bold move.

He rolled to his back, crossing his hands beneath his head, looking up as if he were studying the ceiling. "My father was a mid-level manager for a heavy-equipment firm. The further up the management ladder he climbed, the more he hated what he did. But he earned a good living." He turned his head to look at her. "We had a country club membership, tennis lessons in the summer and my sister and I both had a college education. My parents were very much about keeping up with the Joneses. Not an indictment, just a fact."

She nodded. "My parents are very social conscious, as well." She wrapped her arms around her knees and waited on him to continue.

He picked up the thread. "My dad and I had a standing golf date every Sunday afternoon at the club. There was so much my dad was interested in doing. He was one month away from retirement. Every Sunday, he'd tell me all his big plans for living when he retired." He uttered a humph that was somewhere between a laugh and sigh, shaking his head. "Dad teed off from the seventeenth hole and the ball hooked to the right. Shanking it to the right was something he constantly fought. He groaned and clutched his chest. I thought he was just aggravated." This so was not going to have a happy ending. "He died." Dalton's face took on a hard, closed expression. "Right there. On the spot. He was miserable for thirty-five years and dropped dead before he got the chance to do all of that living he wanted to do."

She nodded sympathetically. She'd seen it firsthand in training. Nonetheless, this was Dalton and his pain and it was so much more personal and intense. She didn't know what to say because nothing she said or did would make it any better. "I'm sure that was hard."

It was his turn to nod. "I left not long after the funeral. Quit my job, cashed in my stocks, sold my condo and my furniture and headed out to do what I wanted to do when I retired. I didn't want to wait until then to live. My mother still hasn't forgiven me. Neither has my former fiancée."

"Fiancée?" She felt as if she'd been kicked in the abdomen. Of course, she hadn't expected that he'd lived in a vacuum but she really hadn't given the women in his life any thought. After all, she herself was simply moving in and out of his life. But now it was staring her in the face. And she really didn't much like it. "You were engaged?"

"That's generally what that tag means."

"Date set?"

"No. Just a ring. I asked her to come with me." The last bit came out with a defensive edge to it.

"You knew she'd say no."

He shrugged. "I can't say I was surprised when Laura passed on trading in a slice of suburban paradise with the prerequisite mortgage, a mini-van and a couple of kids for a life in the Alaskan bush. The truth of the matter was, I was more disappointed than broken-hearted. I told her to keep the ring."

So somewhere out there was a woman who still had an engagement ring from Dalton Saunders. "You didn't owe her that."

"From where I stood, I did. She signed on for one thing and she wound up with another."

Skye felt so weird inside. It took her a moment to realize that she was jealous, which was totally ludicrous. First off, she didn't have a jealous bone in her body—at least she'd never thought she had. Second, she had absolutely no right to experience jealousy of any sort regarding her temporary indulgence. And third, he'd walked away from the woman, so why was she sitting here speculating as to what kind of woman Dalton Saunders would have been engaged to?

"What was she like?" Nothing ventured, nothing gained and her need to know outweighed her need not to ask.

"Looks? Personality? Career?"

What the heck, why not just go for broke? "All of the above."

"Okay, Dr. Nosey."

"I prefer curious."

"Blond, petite, nice smile." Instantly, no contest, no holds barred—Skye hated Laura Whatshername. "Her dad was an orthodontist." Big whoop. "It's always struck me as funny that her parting shot was that I'd be sorry because our kids would have had straight teeth."

"Okay, that is pretty funny. And I guess that says plenty about her personality." She just couldn't keep the bitchy comment bottled up inside.

"Just as a matter of general interest, does your family offer gratis brain surgery to family members?"

She knew he was teasing. Nonetheless something inside her fluttered at his question. "I don't believe the issue has ever arisen." She absolutely couldn't stop the next question that came out of her mouth. "What kind of career did Laura have?"

"Elementary school teacher. She was going to stay home with the kids and then when the youngest started school, she was going to go back to teaching."

Ah, a flexible career. "And all of that simply flew out the window for you? In the blink of an eye, it wasn't what you wanted?"

"It was never what I wanted. It was what I was *supposed* to want. It was what I was supposed *to do*."

Skye felt a spark of recognition inside her at the distinction. "So you don't want children?"

"I didn't say that. I think a couple of rugrats with the right person would be good. I just didn't want The Plan with Laura. What about you?"

As a kid growing up, Skye's nanny had watched endless episodes of *The Family Feud*. In the words of the game show host, *Good answer, good answer.* "I don't want The Plan with Laura, either."

"Did you just make a joke, Shanahan?"

She wrinkled her nose and nudged his leg with her toe. "Don't look so surprised."

He grinned. "Okay, okay, I'm not surprised." There was a seriousness in his eyes. "Do you want kids? Wait, let me guess, everyone in your family is expected to contribute to the genius gene pool."

She could take offense but what was the point because he was dead on. "Pretty much."

"What are you, Shanahan? Twenty-eight?"

"Twenty-nine."

"Let me guess, your folks are having a duck because you're not married yet."

He hadn't even bothered to pose it as a question, he was that certain. And he was right.

"You've pegged them."

"And they really thought you'd hit it off with Doc Morrow, didn't they?"

"You have no idea what a guilt trip my mother can lay on you."

"My mother teaches a course in rendering maternal guilt. So, you never said whether you wanted kids."

"I like being a doctor. I'd like to think I'm good at it. I don't want to give up my career to be a mom but I don't want a nanny to raise my kids. Been there, done that and a nanny isn't a parent."

"So, you're looking for a Mr. Mom? That's not going to work now, is it? I'm sure the family expects you to marry a doctor or better yet, a surgeon."

"Did you visit once and I just forgot?" She laughed but it wasn't particularly funny. "Yes, the expectation is that Shanahans will pursue a medical career and a medical mate."

"And what if a medical mate isn't what makes a Shanahan happy?"

"Fulfilling obligations makes a Shanahan happy."

"No room for abdication of obligation, eh?"

"None, whatsoever."

"So, do you always do what your parents want?"

That made her sound like a doormat. "No. I don't always do what they want."

He tugged at one of the curls her hair had relaxed into. "You're here in Alaska, aren't you, honey?"

"But I didn't hook up with Dr. Morrow, did I?"

He got that look in his eyes and cupped her shoulder in his hand. "No, you hooked up with me." He leaned in and nuzzled her neck. "Just think how much your parents would disapprove."

She almost got the impression that he wanted her to pipe up and tell him they wouldn't disapprove that much. But she didn't, because they would. "They'd be horrified."

She brightened at an idea. He'd already surprised her once and nothing was as it seemed here in Alaska. "Unless you've got a secret geneticist degree or something you haven't mentioned."

"Sorry, honey. Just your standard run of the mill bush pilot with an accounting degree and a CPA status that's now defunct."

"Right."

"Most parents thought I was a catch."

He had absolutely no concept of just how formidable Clan Shanahan could be. "Mine aren't most parents."

14

Thursday evening, a week later, Dalton crossed the short expanse of airfield from his plane to the air center. He checked out what was happening through the big windows overlooking the airstrip on his way to the door.

The office held the usual consortium of Good Riddance residents. Dwight and Jeb sat over by the stove, engrossed in checkers and world politics, no doubt. Clint stood nursing a cup of coffee and talking with Merrilee while his malamute Kobuk lay curled in a ball in front of the stove.

Everything was normal and as it should be, except farther down the street, Skye Shanahan waited. Just thinking about her made him smile, step lighter, and feel all hot and full inside. He'd damn sure never met someone like her before and he doubted he ever would again. A woman like Skye Shanahan only crossed a man's path once in a lifetime.

When he opened the airstrip door, the heat, along

with Merrilee and Clint, greeted him. He and Clint shook hands.

"How's it going with your Japanese scientist?" Dalton said.

"Extremely well. Research wise, he's hit the jackpot." Clint nodded in the direction of the connecting door that muted the noise of Gus's on the other side. "He's chowing down at Gus's now. Pretty interesting fellow but I'm glad to give it a break." Clint grinned. "He was so damn glad to find out I really did speak Japanese, he's talked my ear off this week."

Both Merrilee and Dalton laughed at Clint's cha-grined expression. "I'm sure he was thrilled to have someone to talk to," Merrilee said.

"Thrilled about covers it." Clint nodded to the up-stairs area that housed the bed portion of Merrilee's bed and breakfast. "And considering that Dr. Yamaguchi is staying with me—" he shook his head "—well, let's just say I'm glad he's over at Gus's now." Clint had wound up offering his client accommodations since the town B&B was temporarily out of commission. He glanced at Dal-ton. "How's it going with your boarder?" He frowned. "I heard about Culpepper."

Of course he had. It was bound to get around. Such was the way of things in Good Riddance. "Culpepper or not, I definitely got the better boarder."

"There's no denying that."

Dalton handed over his flight paperwork to Merrilee. "Speaking of Skye, I'd better be heading over to the clinic. She should be finished by now and the woman gets cranky when she's hungry."

He was just kidding and they all knew it. He was simply ready to see her. They'd stayed with the pattern established on the first day. Dalton walked over in the evening and together they strolled over to Gus's for dinner and a drink before heading out to Shadow Lake.

Clint finished the rest of his coffee. "I'm about to grab some dinner myself. Just thought I'd give Yamaguchi some time to make new friends in the bar before I headed over."

Nodding in sympathy, Dalton looked over at Merrilee. "We'll see you there in a few, too."

Merrilee shook her head. "I can't close down yet. Got a call from Anchorage that a private charter is arriving in about an hour and a half."

Dalton whistled under his breath. "Private charter. Big money there. Where are they gonna stay?"

"I told them we couldn't offer accommodations and they said that wouldn't be a problem. The client has their own private room lined up."

They all exchanged a speculative glance. Merrilee shook her head. "Nope. Haven't heard a word from anyone."

Usually if someone had friends or family coming in, it was big news. Clint shrugged. "Oh, well. I guess we'll know in a couple of hours, huh?"

Dalton reached for the clipboard, more interested in finding out what his day looked like tomorrow than the town's unexpected visitor. All he cared about was getting the hell out of dodge and going to pick up Skye. It was kind of crazy how much he wanted to see her.

Within a few minutes he and Merrilee had wrapped up their business and he was walking in the clinic door.

Nelson glanced to the front door to see who was coming in. Dalton waved a greeting. "How's it going Nelson?" Then he clicked the lock in place behind him. Nelson left the door unlocked for Dalton and Dalton locked up when he came in every evening, otherwise people would continue to drift in and out, regardless of whether the office was officially closed or not.

"Busy day as usual, but all's well. How about you?"

Dalton slapped Nelson on the back as he passed him to walk into Skye's office. "Can't complain." He nodded to Skye who sat on the other side of the desk. "Doc."

Damn if he didn't knot up inside just seeing her. She nodded a greeting back. "Dalton. Glad to see you made it back today so I've got a ride home tonight." Her saucy grin turned him inside out.

Nelson laughed, reminding Dalton that they weren't alone. For one crazy-ass second, he'd forgotten everything and everyone else. "I'm heading over to Gus's. I'll save the two of you a seat in the front."

Dalton nodded. "Clint's over there. I just ran into him at the airstrip."

A perplexed look on her face, Skye glanced from one to the other. "Save us a seat in the front? We usually sit in that booth over on the other side of the bar." The booth they'd been in when Little John had started the fight.

"But it's the second Thursday of the month," Nelson said. "That's karaoke night. It'll be packed and you'll want a good seat."

"That's sweet of you, Nelson. But I'll pass. I'm not much on karaoke."

Dalton knew her well enough to read her meaning behind those polite words. Karaoke was probably right up there with shoving a hot poker in her eye. Nelson, however, would handle this one.

Nelson, indeed, gave her his I'm-the-shaman-in-training smile that sort of led people to believe he had some kind of psychic/mystical inside track. "I'll save you a seat. You can't leave Good Riddance without attending karaoke night."

She sighed, closing the chart in front of her, obviously capitulating. "Fine. Save us a seat down front."

Nodding, Nelson turned on his heel and headed for the front door. "See you there." He flipped off the lights in the waiting room.

Dalton was already bridging the space between them when the front door clicked, announcing they were alone. He took her in his arms and suddenly he was kissing her as if it'd been months instead of hours since he'd last touched her. And there was an equally eager, desperate edge to her kisses as well.

They broke apart and he rested his forehead against hers. "I missed you."

He hadn't meant to say it. The words had just tumbled

out, riding the current of that kiss. "I missed you, too." She brushed her forehead against his.

Another kiss led to yet another and another until they were straining against one another. "Dalton..." She licked his lower lip with the tip of her tongue.

"Yes?"

She turned around and swept aside the stack of charts on top of the desk. She faced him, reached behind her and tugged her hair loose, unlatching the gate on his control.

Perching on the edge of her desk, she wrapped her arms around his neck and pulled him into the vee of her legs. "I can't wait until after dinner. What do you think about having dessert first?"

"I think that's an excellent idea."

Skye looked around Gus's as she finished her glass of wine, seeing proof of Nelson's forecast. "It's almost as crowded as the night I arrived in town," she said to Dalton.

He grinned at her across the booth. "In case you haven't noticed, we're a little short on entertainment here. Karaoke night is a big, big deal."

For a second she lost herself in his eyes, in the flicker of heat that left them both remembering the wickedly good sex they'd shared on her desk. She was turning into a wanton wild woman here in Good Riddance. And quite frankly, she couldn't remember when she'd felt more alive. Take now, for instance. She was sitting in Gus's place with her hair curling like crazy all around her head. She'd run out of time to flat-iron it this morning and had merely scraped it back into a tight bun. She'd started to put it back up before they came to Gus's, but Dalton had stopped her.

"Why not just leave it down? Take a walk on the wild side."

"But I have a professional image."

"You've got one more day at the clinic, Skye. In the first place, none of your patients care whether your hair is up or down. Anyway, you're leaving on Saturday. What difference does it make?"

She'd pushed aside the ache the thought of leaving engendered and embraced the idea of letting her hair down, literally and figuratively.

"Penny for them," Dalton said, his voice low, a smile curving his lips, but his eyes were serious.

She shook her head, leaving her reverie behind. "What?"

"A penny for your thoughts."

She laughed, "You'd be short-changed." Nelson caught her eye from across the room. "I suppose we'd better go join Nelson before a riot starts over him saving us two primo seats for the big event."

"Probably a good idea. It doesn't take much to set this crowd off sometimes."

"You go on over. I'm stopping by the bar. I'll need another glass of wine if I'm going to sit through this."

Instead of going on over, however, Dalton stopped off at the bar with her. "Got a question for you."

She ordered her second glass of chardonnay. "Okay."

"Have you ever actually hung out when karaoke was going on?"

He *so* had her number. "Well, no. It just never sounded like my thing."

"I'm thinking it wasn't quite high-brow enough."

She opened her mouth to deny it, but that was pretty much the bottom line. Skye had actually loved singing along with CDs in her room when she was a teenager, pretending she was some out-there rock star. She'd been rocking out one day when her mother—God only knows why her mother had been at home that afternoon rather than in surgery or at the office—had come in and looked at her as if she'd grown another head. Her mother had informed her she was wasting time, that she should be studying. God, she could still remember the song— Sheryl Crow's "All I Wanna Do." She hated that song to this day.

"It just always struck me as a waste of time."

"Well, honey, we've got nowhere to go and no place in particular to be, so just relax." He leaned in close to her ear. "I think you just might enjoy it."

She snagged her wine. Dalton sometimes scared her with how well he seemed to know the person she kept from the rest of the world. "Stranger things have happened."

Placing his hand on the small of her back, he ushered her through the crowded tables to where Nelson, Clint, Bull, Donna and a guy she thought was a prospector named Pete all sat.

"Merrilee still waiting on that charter?" Dalton asked Bull.

"Yep. There was a delay on it leaving Vancouver, so it's going to be getting in later than expected."

"Did anyone ever show up to meet whoever's coming in?" Donna said.

Skye had never actually met a transgender before. Donna, who'd fallen into the habit of coming over for an early morning coffee, cinnamon roll and the latest gossip was as nice as could be. Skye was finally getting to the point where she sort of forgot that Donna used to be Don. Skye sure as heck envied Donna's flawless skin. No freckles there.

"Nope." Bull shook his massive head.

"Looks like Good Riddance has a mystery visitor showing up," Prospector Pete said. Skye noticed Pete and Donna were holding hands. That was nice. Good for them.

Everyone exchanged a look and then Bull elbowed Nelson. "You ready?"

With a nod, Nelson got to his feet and bounded up onto the small stage set back into the corner. He stepped up to the microphone, "Okay, everybody ready to get this party started?"

The crowd roared.

"I can't hear you," he called back in a sing-song voice.

The crowd grew even louder. Meanwhile, Skye sat there in a state of veritable shock. Nelson? Quiet, soft-spoken, shaman-in-training Nelson was the karaoke emcee? She took a gulp of her wine and glanced at Dalton who merely grinned at her obvious surprise.

"Nelson loves this," he said, leaning over so she could hear him. "And he's good at it."

Nelson grabbed the microphone off the stand and pranced across the stage. "So, we're going to start off a little different tonight since Merrilee is still working. But she's promised she and Bull will be up here before the night is over, hitting you with their own version of Sonny and Cher's 'I've Got You Babe.'"

That announcement set off a round of cheering and whistling. Okay, she was glad she'd stayed because she, for one, wanted to see the massively built Bull Swenson up on stage singing Sonny Bono's part. She just couldn't imagine it.

"I hear ya. But tonight yours truly is going to start us off. How about giving it up for a little Smokey Robinson and 'Cruisin.'"

OMG. She polished off the rest of her wine almost absentmindedly. And then she was caught up in the fever. Nelson had a great voice.

"You want a glass of water?" Dalton asked.

By God, for once she was going to let her hair down. She only had one more day in Good Riddance and she didn't think anyone in this room would give a rat's ass—wow, it felt good to think that phrase—if Dr. Skye Shanahan actually had another glass of wine.

"Nah. I'll take another chardonnay."

"Okay, then. Coming right up."

She clapped just as loud as everyone else when Nelson

finished. Who'd have ever guessed he was such a ham beneath that quiet facade. He bowed in three directions and then said, "Thank ya, thank ya vera much," in a very bad Elvis imitation which was funny nonetheless.

Three songs and her third glass of wine later, Skye was totally into it. She swayed and clapped and laughed and was generally having about the best time she could ever remember having...well, other than when she was busy getting all hot and sweaty with Saunders.

"Okay, people, last sign-up on the sheet is Donna and then we're going to go open mike. Put your hands together for Donna singing 'You Make Me Feel Like a Natural Woman.'"

Skye really listened to and absorbed the words of the song as Donna got up and sang in front of the crowd, but directly to Pete. It was touching and brave and...well, inspiring. Donna returned to the table and Nelson went back to emceeing. "Okay, folks, who's up next? Who's got a song inside them just waiting to get out?"

Skye didn't hesitate. She just reacted, standing up and saying, "Me."

Nelson's grin nearly split his face. "Alright then. We've got Dr. Skye taking to the stage."

She couldn't resist looking over her shoulder at Dalton. His smile was equally big and approving. "You go, baby."

Turning back around, Skye paused for a second. Did she really want to do this? Had she had too much to drink? Would she regret this in the morning? Yes, she did. No, she hadn't. And no, she wouldn't regret it in the morning. She made her way to the stage and gave Nelson her song of choice.

"We can hook you up with that."

Hook her up? Nelson was definitely a different human being in deejay mode.

He handed her the microphone and she looked out over the crowd, adrenalin surging through her. The opening chords to Bonnie Raitt's 'Something to Talk About' came over the sound system and Skye felt exhilarated and powerful and free. She launched into the song, singing it directly to Dalton the way Donna had sung to Pete. And she didn't hold back. As she sang, she danced and flirted with him and generally threw herself into what would probably be her one and only onstage performance ever.

The song ended and the room erupted with clapping. She was most gratified to see Dalton jump to his feet, clapping loud and hard. Feeling absolutely on top of the world, she was about to hand the microphone back to Nelson when she looked all the way to the back of the room.

No. Not possible. She closed her eyes and slowly reopened them. Okay, she didn't think she was drunk but clearly she was hallucinating. There was Merrilee in the back of the room and next to her was… God, please let the person next to Merrilee be a hallucination.

Skye realized the room had grown quiet as a church while Nelson stood next to her awkwardly waiting on her to relinquish the microphone. She would, just as soon as she gave herself a sanity—or sobriety—check.

"Mother?" Skye's voice seemed to echo around the room over the sound system.

"Skye Shanahan, what do you think you're doing?" Each word, uttered in her mother's precise, disapproving tone, seemed to fire through the room like a volley.

"It's called singing, Mother. More specifically karaoke."

And then she did something she'd never done in public and certainly hadn't planned to now, but it just happened. Dr. Skye Shanahan burped into the microphone.

15

DAMAGE CONTROL WAS Dalton's first thought as he rounded the table to meet Skye as she came off the stage. He wasn't leaving her to face that woman alone. Nelson had the good sense to pull out the one thing that would distract the crowd.

"Well, it looks like Merrilee is here now, so she and Bull are up next."

Skye stepped off the stage and Dalton held out his hand, locking his gaze with hers, telling her he'd face the dragon with her or respect her privacy if that's what she preferred. "Do you want some company?" he asked in a low undertone.

"Are you sure you want to do this?" Which translated roughly to *you must be crazy.*

"I've got your back."

She put her hand in his. "Thanks, Saunders."

"Don't mention it, Shanahan."

He could feel the tension radiating off her as they moved through the crowd. But it was slow going as everyone had to give her an "attagirl" on her way to the back of the room. He hoped she realized it was also the town's way of telling her that they had her back as well. She may have only been here for eleven days, but she had cared for them and their children, given advice, medicine and sympathy when it was needed. In the eyes of the town, she was one of them now. And Good Riddance took care of their own.

They passed Merrilee halfway through the crowd as she was making her way to join Bull on stage. Nelson was continuing to fill the silence with deejay chatter and the crowd was back to talking and laughing amongst themselves. Merrilee paused briefly, putting a hand on Skye's arm. "Honey, if I'd known, I would've given you a heads up."

Skye nodded and patted Merrilee's hand as if to reassure the older woman. "I know. It's not a problem." Skye turned toward the stage. "Now you better go before the crowd gets out of control. You know how easy that happens around here."

Merrilee smiled. "That I do." Dalton didn't miss the faint nod of approval Merrilee sent his way, one that said he was doing the right thing to go with Skye.

As they spanned the rest of the distance, Dalton took stock of her mother. Slightly taller than Skye, black hair cut in a stylish bob, porcelain skin and an expensive suit, the only thing that gave away the genetic link between the two women was her mother's intensely blue eyes.

Dalton squeezed Skye's hand in silent reassurance just before they stopped in front of the other woman.

"Mother," Skye greeted, neither of them making a move to hug one another.

He and his mother might only see each other once a year—and it had taken his mom nearly five years to forgive him for moving to Alaska—but they always met each other with a hug.

"This is Dalton Saunders. Dalton, this is my mother, Dr. Patrice Shanahan."

The woman's shrewd blue eyes missed nothing. She took in Skye's hand clasped in his and no doubt noticed that he needed a haircut. Releasing Skye, he extended his hand to the older Dr. Shanahan. Hesitating briefly, she finally accepted his greeting with a shake.

"Pleased to meet you, Dr. Shanahan." It wasn't strictly the truth but he felt that Skye would be better served by his good manners rather than veracity at this point.

"Hello. And exactly who are you?"

Skye spoke up. "Dalton is a friend." She reclaimed his hand with her own.

Her mother's nostrils flared slightly. "So I gathered from that…display, up there."

Skye raised her chin slightly, her tone echoing her mother's. "What are you doing here, Mother?"

"I'm speaking at a conference in Vancouver that starts tomorrow afternoon. Since I was in the neighborhood, relatively speaking, I thought I'd drop in and meet Janine's son. Where is Dr. Morrow?" There was no mistaking her emphasis on Morrow's title.

"I have no clue, Mother. He was gone when I arrived and I assume he'll be back after I've left."

The woman was all stern disapproval. "But Janine said he was going to spend his vacation at home, hunting and fishing."

"Janine will have to take that up with him. All I can tell you about Dr. Morrow is that he has deplorable taste. He's painted yellow flowers all over the clinic walls. Still, they're beginning to grow on me."

"Is that supposed to be a joke?" Mama clearly wasn't amused.

"You know I never joke, Mother."

Dalton knew that to be a lie, but he was sure that she did never joke around this woman. On the stage, Merrilee and Bull were singing. Dr. Shanahan cut her eyes in that direction and then back to her daughter.

"I've had enough. I'm ready to go."

"Go? You're heading back to Vancouver tonight?"

Hope could only spring eternal.

"Don't be ridiculous. Of course not. I'm staying with you tonight. I thought we could share your accommodations for one evening. It will give us a chance to catch up. My flight leaves mid-morning."

Oh, boy.

"That's going to be a bit awkward, Mother."

"Awkward in what respect, Skye?"

Enough. He'd take a turn under fire. Dalton spoke up. "The rooms at the Bed and Breakfast are out of commission. There are two cabins out at my property. There's a problem with the shower in the empty cabin and then there was a security incident. Skye's been staying with me."

"I see." And Mrs. Shanahan did. Clearly. Disdain and disapproval rolled off her in waves. "I suppose it's a good thing you're getting this out of your system here." *Where no one knows you and we won't all be embarrassed.* Sometimes the things left unspoken came through more loudly than the things said. "And your hair is a mess."

Skye squared her shoulders. "I like it."

"I'm ready to go," Skye's mother said.

Back straight, shoulders square, her daughter faced her down. "We're not."

It might not have been the smartest move he'd ever made but Dalton took his life in his hands and figuratively stepped between the two of them. "Why don't we get dinner to go. We've already seen the best of the evening, Skye. We can head on out to Shadow Lake."

For a couple of seconds he thought she was going to argue with him, but finally she simply nodded her acquiescence.

"Fine."

It was going to be a damn long ride home tonight.

SKYE SAT SANDWICHED IN THE truck's front seat between Dalton and her mother. He had been a lifesaver tonight. Leaning slightly into him, she absorbed his warmth and his unflagging support of her.

Her mother broke the silence stretching uncomfortably between them. "You know your father and I only want the best for you, Skye."

"Yes, I know, Mother." She answered by rote. She'd

been hearing that same thing all of her life. She didn't doubt her parents' sincerity. In their own way, they loved her just as they loved Patrick and Bridgette also. But suddenly Skye had a new take on things. She chose her words carefully. "I truly do know that, Mother. But it's your idea of the best. And what's best for you and Dad isn't necessarily what's best for me."

"We respected that when you opted not to specialize. But we are older with life experience behind us."

"I understand that and I appreciate it. But I'm not a child anymore. I've got a little life experience behind me as well, Mother."

Skye wasn't surprised at all when her mother ignored that and blithely changed the subject. "Bridgette and Donald are throwing a little dinner party next weekend to welcome you back home. They thought it would be fun for everyone to hear about your stint in the Alaskan wilds."

Beside her, Dalton stiffened, his shoulder rigid against her own. "How nice," Skye said. It was a lame response but she could hardly announce that she wasn't going to attend a dinner party in her honor—mainly because there was no reason for her not to go. Sounding churlish and childish would hardly further her argument that she was now an adult capable of directing her own life and making her own sound decisions.

Mercifully the headlights picked out the turn to Shadow Lake. "Here we are. Welcome to Shadow Lake."

For Skye, there was a measure of homecoming in

the towering spruce lining the unpaved driveway that then gave way to the clearing on the lake's edge where moonlight danced across the water. She hadn't felt that way a week ago or even a day ago, but tonight a comfort and sense of belonging swept through her as they pulled up to park in front of the two cabins.

Dalton, obviously sensing that she and her mother had said what they needed to say, broke into the story of the two sisters from Idaho who'd made Shadow Lake their home after retirement. He was actually a good storyteller, Skye realized, as he showed her mother Ms. Irene's cabin. He even managed to work in the cabin-to-cabin contact system.

He paused at the bathroom door. "I'm afraid there's a problem with the shower."

"As long as there's running water, I'll manage. I showered this morning and I can shower when I return to the hotel tomorrow."

"Okay then. Just pick up the phone if you have a problem."

Skye dreaded what she knew was about to come. She headed to the front door with Dalton. "Night, Mother."

"What? You're not staying here with me?"

She'd had a lifetime with her mother and when she went back to Atlanta, she'd have plenty of time with her then as well. But she had two more nights with this man. "No. I'm not staying here with you. I'm staying next door with him."

Her mother eyed Dalton up and down and promptly

dismissed him. It was insulting and while Skye couldn't control her mother's expressions, she could stop a tirade before it started. "Don't. Not a word. We'll see you in the morning."

Her mother did manage, however, to get the last word in. As they closed the door behind them, they heard the words, "Temporary insanity."

Dalton slipped an arm around her. "Thank you," she said, "for everything."

"You're welcome." He opened the cabin door and she'd never been so happy to be anywhere before in her life. "I'll start the fire if you'll turn on the lamp."

Silently, they each set about doing their thing. Skye had always found her parents fairly intimidating—their demeanor, their brains, their success. But tonight, for the first time in her life, she saw her mother differently. Dr. Patrice Shanahan would certainly have a meltdown if she even had an inkling of what Skye thought. Because for the first time in her life, she was embarrassed by her mother.

She moved around the room, full of nervous energy. Finally, she looked at Dalton squatting before the fire, patiently coaxing the flames. "Go ahead and say something."

He looked at her over his shoulder. "Wow." He offered that grin that always made her want to smile in return. "That explains a lot. And you were magnificent, by the way." He left the hearth and crossed the room to her. "I never got a chance to tell you, but you were great on the karaoke too. That was hot. You were hot."

She was fairly certain no one had ever used the term hot in conjunction with herself. He couldn't have possibly said anything more perfect at this point in time.

"Really?"

"Really."

She read the flicker of heat in his eyes, felt the desire in his touch and she also saw him wrestle with himself to try and be a sensitive male. "Do you need to talk about tonight? Your mother?"

She loved him. She was in love with him. The knowledge had been dancing around her, through her for the last week and she'd steadfastly ignored it, as if it would change things. But there was no denying it to herself any longer. If she hadn't already been in love with him, tonight would've sealed the deal. He obviously wanted to have sex, yet he was offering to do the one thing most men ran hard and fast from—talking, and about her mother, even.

She stroked his face with her fingertips, loving the feel of his whiskers against her skin. "That is really sweet of you to offer, but no, I do not want to talk about my mother." She fitted her hips against his and pressed against him. "I want to get naked with you."

He cupped her derriere in his big hands and pulled her harder against him. "Well, if that's what you really want..."

It was most definitely what she really wanted.

THE CLOCK SAID 2:00 A.M. AND Dalton could tell by her breathing that Skye was still awake. He couldn't seem to sleep either. Outside the cabin, a wolf's cry echoed across the lake. Almost immediately a second one answered.

"I like to hear the wolves," he said. "I always wonder what they're saying."

"Probably something along the line of 'hey, quit star-gazing and come to bed.'" Smiling at her joke, he rolled over and wrapped his arm about her middle, pulling her tighter against him. She stroked his arm. "What does it feel like that this all belongs to you?" she said.

"It doesn't, you know, not really."

"But you said Irene Marbut left Shadow Lake to you." Perplexity came through her voice.

"She did. But I tend to buy into the way the natives see it, that we can never really own the land. I'd like to think of myself as more of a steward, a protector." In his mind's eye he could see the mountains that ringed the property and he told her what he hadn't told anyone else. "I didn't want it."

She shifted and studied him in the faint light cast by the glowing embers. "Why not? I've always had the impression that you loved it here."

"I do. And I loved Ms. Irene the same way I love my family. I know she thought she was doing me a favor but I don't want to be tied to Shadow Lake."

She nodded and traced her finger over his left pec. "You have real issues about not being tied anywhere, don't you?"

"It's not as extreme as you make it sound. It's beauti-ful here and I do like my privacy, but Shadow Lake is too remote, too isolated, even for me. Irene and Erlene had each other. And then Irene and I had each other. I've discovered I wasn't cut out to be a hermit." He hesitated, and then told her how he felt. "It's been nice having you here these last two weeks."

"Glad I could fill that space for you, Saunders." That prickliness it had taken him forever to move past made a return appearance.

"Don't, Shanahan."

"Don't what?"

"Just don't. You know you've been more than a space filler." Before he was tempted to say something really stupid that could only lead nowhere, he said the practical thing. "I didn't like her, Skye."

She knew who he was talking about. "I know. Sometimes she's not very likeable." He was inclined to think that was about ninety-nine point nine percent of the time but he kept his mouth shut. "She didn't like you, either."

"No, she didn't. No big surprise there, though."

"No."

"The rest of your family?"

"My father and mother are well-suited." Damn, he was sorry to hear that. "Patrick is smart and ambitious. Bridgette is all about serving on club committees as is befitting a surgeon's wife."

God, how did she even stand a chance? She'd stood up to her mother last night, while she was here and had his support and the people of Good Riddance backing her. But who would be in her corner when she got back to Georgia? This wasn't about him or even the two of them, this was about her.

He was really about to wade into the fray and he suspected it wasn't going to go well with her. He knew it was a damn sensitive subject. Nonetheless, it needed to be said. "Don't let them run your life, Skye. You've got to stand up for what you want and who you are."

"How would you begin to know who I am and what I want?" She wasn't happy but her tone wasn't nearly as defensive or hostile as he'd anticipated.

"I'm going to give it to you straight," he said. "When I met you in Anchorage, you were damn near a replica of your mother." Amazing that what seemed like a lifetime was actually less than two weeks ago. "But there was something else there, a spark, a fire that your mother doesn't have. Everything inside me tells me that the woman who sang on that stage tonight is the real Skye Shanahan. It'll be a damn shame if your family can't appreciate that woman, as well."

"It's not as easy as you make it sound. And not everyone can simply up and walk away from their life."

"It depends on how badly you want another life."

"How much better off are you, Dalton? True, you're not weighed down by a corporate job with a wife, two kids and a mortgage, but in a way you're weighed down by your resolve to be tied to nothing. And in the end, you may wind up with just that—nothing. It seems a pretty high price to pay."

They lay there together until the alarm went off announcing a new day, but there was nothing left to say.

16

SATURDAY MORNING SKYE HELPED Dalton load the last of her luggage into the back of his pickup. The last twenty-four hours had passed in a flash. Her mother had left Friday morning without any further commentary other than she'd see Skye back in Atlanta next week.

And where she'd been swamped with patients her first week because all the men wanted a chance to meet her, on Friday she'd been overrun with people wanting to wish her well, with more than a few telling her not to let her mother get the best of her. A week ago she would have found the familiarity offensive, yesterday she'd simply found it touching.

Neither she nor Dalton had mentioned the conversation they'd had in the dark, small hours of the morning.

"Ready?" he said.

She opened her mouth to respond but found speech impossible with tears clogging her throat. So, she merely nodded, jamming her sunglasses into place even though the sun was fairly weak today. She took one final look at the lake and mountains and the two cabins nestled side-by-side against the backdrop of spruce trees, and her heart literally ached in her chest.

It was as if something very real and vital inside her was being ripped out. But this wasn't her world. For a brief period of time she'd found a portion of herself here, but she'd been told from the time she was a child where she belonged and it wasn't here.

The thought of never seeing Dalton again was nearly unbearable. "I don't suppose you ever get down to the lower forty-eight."

"Sure I do. I do the holiday thing with my family pretty much every year. They're in Lansing."

"Michigan, right?"

"Yeah."

"That's a long way from Atlanta but hey, if you ever have a bush pilot conference or something there, look me up."

They both knew there weren't bush pilot conferences. And if there were, they certainly wouldn't be in Atlanta.

"You know, if you decide to come back for a vacation, just to do the tourist thing, let me know. Pop a couple of motion sickness pills and I can give you an amazing aerial tour. In a month, the northern lights will be spectacular. And summers are something else."

"I don't have any vacation time for another year."

"That would make it difficult for you to get up here, then."

She was, quite suddenly, exasperated with both of them. This conversation was stupid. They were dancing all around each other without saying what needed to be said. Well, she couldn't speak for him, but she could speak for herself. What difference did it make? She was about to get on a plane and fly more than three thousand miles away. It wasn't as if it would be awkward when she bumped into him in the grocery store.

"Saunders, these have been two of the best weeks of my life and a large part of that has been because of you."

"Shanahan, I feel the same way."

Something warm and wonderful blossomed inside her at his words. Okay, then. That much was out of the way. She waited…and waited…for more. Several times during the rest of the trip to Good Riddance, she thought he was on the verge of saying something else, but silence reigned. And she had nothing left to say.

They pulled up at the airstrip. Dalton looked straight ahead. "There's been a little change in plans. Juliette will be flying you on to Anchorage."

Skye felt winded, as if she'd taken a fall and had the breath knocked out of her. She knew she was leaving. She knew it was goodbye but she thought she'd at least have the plane ride to Anchorage with him. Hot tears gathered behind her eyes and clogged her throat. She pushed them back.

She. Would. Not. Cry.

"Oh," she said, when she could once again speak. "I see."

What should she say to him? What did she want to say to him? What did you say to a man who was totally inappropriate when you had foolishly fallen in love with him in two weeks? That was simply not the kind of thing Shanahans did.

"Well, best of luck with everything," she finally said.

"You, too."

She thought about hugging him or shaking his hand, but in the end she simply opened the door and got out of the truck. She was fairly certain she couldn't touch him without falling apart. She was halfway to the airstrip door when he called out to her.

"Shanahan."

Her heart thumping madly in her chest, she turned. "Yes?"

He stood by his truck, holding a suitcase in each hand. "Take care."

She hesitated, waiting for something more. When nothing was forthcoming, she simply nodded, closer to tears than ever. "You, too."

Her back ramrod straight, she put one foot in front of the other until she was inside the airstrip. Walking in, she got the surprise of her life. It looked as if half the population of Good Riddance was packed inside— apparently all waiting for her. Gus and Merrilee stood at the desk next to a huge cake with Thank You Dr. Skye inscribed on the top of it.

"We couldn't let you leave without a farewell party," Merrilee said.

Donna stepped forward. "Every karaoke night, we give an award for the evening. The crowd votes on it. Sort of a Good Riddance Oscar if you will. Well, you won. And we thought it'd make a nice memento of your time here." The blond woman handed Skye a fake gold-plated toy microphone.

While she was still standing there feeling over-whelmed, Merrilee handed her a wrapped package. "This is from me."

Skye carefully removed the bow and the gift wrap to find a lace-trimmed green and pink flannel shirt inside. She was in serious danger of crying. "It's beautiful."

"I thought the colors would complement your hair and complexion."

And then Nelson presented her with a CD recording of native flute music. Bull stepped forward with a loon carving. Donna had knitted her a hat and matching scarf. Gus had bound a private collection of her recipes for preparing wildlife gourmet dishes. Gus smiled ruefully and shrugged. "I doubt you'll have a big source of fresh moose or caribou available in Atlanta, but I thought you might enjoy it anyway."

Skye could only stand there, feeling slightly over-whelmed. When she'd been leaving Atlanta to spend the week in Good Riddance, no one had given a damn. Some of her office staff and a couple of her colleagues had offered a perfunctory *Have a good trip,* but none of them had actually cared. And she was double certain none of them had missed her unless it was the inconvenience of having her out of the office. No one back *home* cared the way everyone in this room cared.

But none of that mattered because Atlanta was where she belonged.

A WEEK LATER, DALTON WALKED into the air strip center at the end of his day.

"You look miserable," Merrilee said without preamble.

"Thanks. I appreciate that." Miserable about summed it up. He'd always been happy when he was up in his plane. Not now. Likewise, Shadow Lake brought him no peace nor pleasure these days. And dammit to hell, it was all because Skye Shanahan was gone…and she wasn't coming back.

"I could say I told you so," Merrilee said, "but I don't think that's necessary."

"I think you just did."

"And I don't suppose you need for me to point out to you the source of your misery, do you?"

It was one of those rare occasions when the airstrip office was empty except for him and Merrilee. He paced over to the wood stove.

"Damn Shanahan. She ruined this place for me. I thought I'd found just what I was looking for and she's ruined it."

"No, you left behind what you needed to leave behind eight years ago, but you just found what you were looking for. Everyone's running from something and to something. You figured out your *from* something a long time ago, but Dr. Skye is your *to* something."

There was something about Merrilee's expression that, for one fleeting moment, gave him the impression she was still running. Then he dismissed the notion, focusing on the mess that was now his life. He scrubbed his hand through his hair. "It wouldn't work, Merrilee. Her mother pretty much hated me and the feeling was mutual. Skye's a doctor. She's got a bright future ahead of her with some neurosurgeon in a mini-mansion down in Atlanta. And she doesn't like Alaska."

"I'm not sure that's the case anymore, Dalton. I'd like to think she'd grown rather fond of the town and all of us by the time she left."

He shrugged.

She cocked her head to one side and gave him a speculative look. "I tell you what. Just do one thing, if you can."

"What's that?"

"Tell me you don't love that girl. Tell me that the idea of not ever seeing her again, of her settling for someone who doesn't love her like you do, isn't tearing you apart."

He couldn't tell her that because he wasn't going to lie anymore. Not to Merrilee and not to himself. All week he'd refused to face it, deal with it, put a name to it but now Merrilee had dragged it out into the open.

"I do love her. But I can't be what her family needs me to be."

"Nobody asked you to. You only need to be what

she needs and I think that's you, just the way you are. But you've got to be willing to step up to the plate for her. Everyone needs someone in their corner and Skye's someone is you."

He shook his head. "I don't know…."

Merrilee held her hands up, in a gesture of surrender. It was unlike Merrilee to drop something so easily but he appreciated her letting it go. "Well, it is what it is, as my mother, God rest her soul, used to say. Now, what with you being an upstanding citizen of Good Riddance and in my official capacity of mayor, I'd like to ask you to put on your civic duty hat and head up a committee."

"A committee?" What the…? He didn't do committees. And the only thing coming up was the Northern Lights festival, and Nelson's cousin, Luellen Sisnuket, co-chaired that with Donna every year. But when Merrilee asked for something, refusing was never an option. Besides, it would give him something to focus on, other than just how hauntingly lonely the cabin was without Skye.

"Doc Morrow gave me his official resignation today. He's moving. He's trying to decide between Portland and San Francisco," Merrilee said. "Anyway, I'd like for you to chair the committee to find a replacement physician for our fair community."

He had a sudden sensation of his life falling into place, sort of like the moment he realized he was ready to give up his old life and move to Alaska. Only this time, he knew his new life included Skye. "I've got a friend I could ask."

Patting him on the shoulder, Merrilee beamed her approval. "That's kind of what I was thinking. He wants to leave in a month."

"That's not a long time to find a replacement. I'd better get busy."

"Well, the way this works is your committee—and it can be a committee of one if you prefer to work alone—will present a list of qualified candidates to the town council. As Good Riddance's body of elected officials, we'll interview and then vote on the candidates you present."

"How many candidates do I need to present?"

"Oh, one will do." She smiled. "By the way, I used to be with the Junior League Auxillary fund-raiser years ago before The Move. I found that face-to-face recruitment is much more effective than a phone call. Shall I cross you off the air run lists for a few days?"

"Probably a good idea, Merrilee, as I'll be tied up doing my civic duty."

"Dalton?"

"Yes?"

"You might want to get a haircut first." She gave him a wink. "It makes a better first impression."

17

SKYE SWORE UNDER HER BREATH. She'd never been particularly fond of Atlanta traffic—it took a mad person indeed to embrace gridlock—but she'd found it nearly intolerable since her return from Good Riddance. She turned on her CD player and let the soothing flute with the loon's call fill the air. Pulling through the drive-thru at Starbucks, she ordered her usual. Not even that brought her any measure of satisfaction.

She'd dined at one of Atlanta's premier restaurants last night with one of her brother's colleagues. The food hadn't begun to stand up to Gus's and Skye had nearly nodded off during dinner. Sam, she thought his name was Sam, had been dreadfully boring.

She'd had a big epiphany in between the quail with balsamic reduction and the raspberry and white chocolate trifle. On the whole, doctors were a boring lot. She loved practicing medicine and it was interesting to compare notes with other physicians but sometimes you just needed a change of pace, another conversational topic outside of neurologic disorders and the recent performance of a stock portfolio.

She pulled forward to the pickup window and handed over her money in exchange for her venti coffee with sugar and cream and a cinnamon roll. While waiting on her change, she cautiously sipped at the brew. She'd been a tea girl before but Alaska had made her a coffee convert. Nelson actually made a better cup of coffee than this place. And she didn't need to take a bite of the pastry to know it wouldn't begin to measure up to Gus's, either.

She merged into the traffic and it suddenly struck her—she didn't want to be here. She wanted to be in Good Riddance, Alaska. And while she did miss Dalton Saunders with an intensity that wouldn't quit, this wasn't about him. This was about her. She had to get her own life on track before she could think about joining someone else. And where she was now, what she was now, wasn't the right track.

With that one acknowledgment, she felt as if a huge weight had been lifted off of her. She felt liberated—scared as hell, but liberated nonetheless. There were medical positions in Alaska. Barry Morrow had Good Riddance taken care of but there would be openings in Anchorage, Fairbanks, some of the other towns. She'd make it work.

Look at Dalton, Merrilee, Gus, Donna—they'd all done it. Packed up and started over. Would her parents be happy for her? That would be a stretch of the imagination, but what the heck, she'd always fallen slightly short on their approval meter anyway. The idea of facing her parents and breaking the news to them made her slightly nauseous. This was the right thing to do, she could feel it soul-deep, but it wasn't going to be particularly easy.

That was okay. Med school and residency hadn't been particularly easy either. The things worth having in life seldom came without a price.

She mentally began to make a list in her head as she pulled into the office parking lot. She'd tender her resignation—they'd need time to find a replacement. She'd either sell or sub-lease her condo. She'd start putting in applications in Alaska. But the first thing she'd do was give Merrilee a call. There was nothing quite like having a role model who could also give you pointers on how to trade in an old life for a new one.

FRIDAY MORNING DALTON WALKED into the airstrip office. He'd checked in last night and all he had scheduled today was a couple of light runs so he should be able to get that haircut before he headed to Atlanta on Monday.

Jeb and Dwight had already taken up residence in the rocking chairs next to the potbellied stove. Clint was reading the newspaper and sipping a cup of coffee over on the couch, his dog curled up at his feet—both of them, no doubt, waiting on Clint's latest client to make their way downstairs. Dalton and Clint had both pitched in to give Bull a hand repairing the upstairs roof and ceiling.

"Morning, Merrilee," Dalton said, heading straight for the coffee pot. He could use a little caffeine this morning.

"Good morning to you," she said, even bubblier than usual. "I wanted to talk to you about something."

"Shoot."

"Having the upstairs out of commission for that week got me to thinking. How would you feel about me subleasing Irene's cabin from you as an offsite extension of the Good Riddance B&B? It would give me a backup and also offers folks coming in the option of having more of a wilderness experience. But if you think it'll infringe on your privacy, I totally understand."

Since Skye had come and gone, Dalton was more than ready to look into moving into Good Riddance itself. He'd been thinking of building his own house, even though that meant commitment and a mortgage. It no longer felt like a ball and chain anchoring him, perhaps because it was on his terms.

"How would you feel about taking over both of the cabins? I've been knocking around the idea of moving closer to town, maybe building my own place."

"That could work. Let's think about it and we'll come up with something." She handed him his flight schedule. "Juliette's making the short run today. I need you to head down to Anchorage for a package delivery this morning."

He ran his hand over his hair. "I was supposed to get a haircut after the short run. Can't Juliette handle the Anchorage pick-up?"

"Sorry, Dalton. I need you in Anchorage this morning. It's a special package coming in."

Merrilee seldom exasperated him, but she did now. Still, there was nothing he could do. He'd make the run to Anchorage. He was so aggravated he didn't bother to ask what the package was. It had better be damn special to disrupt his plans this way.

SKYE FEARED SHE PRETTY MUCH looked like hell. Cross-country travel could do that to a woman, especially when she'd taken the red-eye out of Atlanta the previous night and had two interminable layovers. That travel schedule, however, had insured she could maximize her long weekend in Good Riddance. And since she had a lot of ground to cover, she needed the time.

Rolling her carry-on behind her, she scanned the faces in Anchorage's airport. Ah, there he was. Just as it had the first time she saw him, her heart began a mad dance in her chest.

The moment he saw her, the moment their eyes locked across the expanse of people, he stood frozen, as if he couldn't quite believe he was seeing her. He shook his head as if he was waking from a dream and then they were both in motion, finding their way to one another as quickly as possible.

Neither said a word as they stepped into each other's arms, their mouths fusing in a kiss of homecoming and welcome.

When they finally broke away, he touched her face tenderly, running his fingers over her forehead down to the curve of her cheek. "Shanahan…Skye…I've missed you. Your hair's down," he said, threading his fingers through her curls. "I love you."

His words were beautifully, wonderfully disjointed and without a doubt, it was the best greeting she'd ever had in her life. "I love you, too, Dalton Saunders."

Someone jostled into her and she became aware once again that they were in the middle of an airport. "Is that plane of yours parked somewhere around here? I'm ready to get to Good Riddance."

"I can get you there. Let's go pick up your luggage and we'll be on our way."

She indicated the carryon behind her. "That's it. I took a lesson or two in figuring out what I really needed."

His gaze was searching. "Then let's go." The rest of the conversation between them was for the privacy of his plane.

Before long, they were cleared for take-off and on their way. "Did you take a motion sickness pill?"

"Done." She grinned at him, her happiness spilling out of her. "I'm not going to throw up in your plane again."

"Good deal." He checked the instrument panel and then looked at her. "I was flying to Atlanta on Monday."

"That's what I heard. I also heard there was a job opening in Good Riddance and it usually works best if you apply in person."

"So I've heard. How'd your parents take the news?"

"How do you think it went over?"

"Pretty bad, huh?"

"In a word, it was horrendous." She smiled and shrugged. "But I haven't been excommunicated from the family, so all's relatively well."

"But I thought your mother wanted you to hook up with Doc Morrow."

"Well, I finally got the whole story. Apparently he'd told his parents he was thinking of moving away from Alaska. They thought if he and I hit it off, it would kill two birds with one stone. He'd move back to Atlanta and we'd be an item. My parents certainly never intended for me to move to Alaska."

"You're certain of this?"

"Absolutely."

"I'm looking for some property closer into town where I can build something."

"You're voluntarily making a commitment, Saunders?"

"Something like that, Shanahan. In fact, I've been thinking about something else, too. You know how things can get around here. I'm thinking I need to put a ring on your finger."

"So, we're back to this whole staking a claim nonsense?"

"Pretty much. It'll just be easier than trying to keep all the poachers at bay. And that's generally what happens when two people decide they love one another and want to have a future together."

"I could do a ring but I don't want to walk down the aisle anytime soon. I want us both to be sure."

"We'll take all the time you need, just as long as it's before the first kid shows up. I'm discovering I'm a little more conventional than I thought."

"This is a bit of a change. I've become the rebel and you've become the stuffed shirt."

He grinned at her. "I have a feeling we'll balance each other back and forth."

"I have a feeling you're right. Now take me home, Saunders."

Epilogue

"WELCOME BACK, AGAIN," Donna said with a hug as the joint welcome back/farewell party got into full swing a month later. Skye hugged the tall blonde back. She had a feeling she and Donna were going to be good friends.

"And you know we're going to miss you," Donna said to Barry Morrow, the other guest of honor. Once Barry and Skye had moved past their mother's futile machinations, they'd realized they liked one another as friends. Considering that Barry was about as gay as they came, that's all it could have ever been. Skye hoped he'd find the wherewithal to come out of the closet sooner rather than later. She knew how liberating it could be to let friends and family know who you really were and then, to move on and live that life. She was nervous, but equally excited that Bridgette had already made plans to fly out in February for Skye's birthday.

The connecting door stood open between the airstrip office and Gus's. Music, conversation, food and drink, and most importantly people flowed between the two establishments.

Skye knew a moment of near-perfect contentment... or she would when Dalton arrived. She scanned the room, anxious for him to get back from his mail run and join the party.

Movement outside the window caught her eye. Her heartbeat accelerated, the same as it always did, the same as it always would, she suspected, as she spotted him crossing the landing strip, heading their way.

Barry sent her a teasing smile. "I see the man of the hour has arrived."

"It's your party. You're the man of the hour," Skye said, teasing him in return.

"True. I guess Dalton's just *your* man of the hour."

"Well, there is that," she said, already stepping away. "If you'll excuse me for a moment."

Moving through the crowd wasn't easy, especially as she was one of the guests of honor. She reached Dalton at the same time as he was delivering the mail to Merrilee, who stood beside the desk.

"Thanks, Dalton," Merrilee said, spilling the bag's contents onto her desk and sorting quickly—rain or shine or party—nothing stopped the mail.

"Hey, you," he said, slipping an arm around her.

"Good flight?"

"Yep. Better now that I'm back for your party."

One moment she and Dalton were standing there talking and the next thing Skye knew, out of the corner of her eye, she saw Merrilee slump into her chair. In seconds, she was at the older woman's side.

"Are you okay?" Skye already had Merrilee's hand in her own, checking her pulse, noting her shallow, rapid breathing.

"I'm fine," Merrilee said, although her smile was weak. Perhaps because she was trained to look for details, Skye saw Merrilee slip a letter back under the stack. She also saw the Georgia postmark peeking out of the corner.

Bull joined them, concern etching the lines on his face even deeper. "What's the matter? What's wrong?"

Merrilee shook off Skye's hand and stood, her usual smile more firmly fixed into place. "Nothing. I'm fine. I guess I shouldn't have skipped breakfast this morning. But knowing we were going to have all of this food…" She waved a hand around them at the party in full swing. "Now I guess I better go make myself a plate before I get woozy again, huh?"

Bull nodded and took her elbow, leading her toward the table, obviously relieved Merrilee was okay.

"What do you think?" Dalton asked in a low tone at Skye's side.

"Later. At home. Now's not the time." What she thought was Merrilee's condition had nothing to do with skipping breakfast. A missed meal didn't produce a mild case of shock. Something in that letter had terribly upset the older woman, but Skye could only respect Merrilee's privacy and offer her a sympathetic ear if she needed someone to talk to.

"Later it is, then," Dalton said. He looked out at the gathering of townspeople crowding the rooms. "Welcome home, Doc."

* * * * *

COMING NEXT MONTH

Available October 26, 2010

HBCNM1010

REQUEST YOUR FREE BOOKS!

2 FREE NOVELS PLUS 2 FREE GIFTS!

HARLEQUIN®

Blaze™

Red-hot reads!

YES! Please send me 2 FREE Harlequin® Blaze™ novels and my 2 FREE gifts (gifts are worth about $10). After receiving them, if I don't wish to receive any more books, I can return the shipping statement marked "cancel." If I don't cancel, I will receive 6 brand-new novels every month and be billed just $4.24 per book in the U.S. or $4.71 per book in Canada. That's a saving of at least 15% off the cover price. It's quite a bargain. Shipping and handling is just 50¢ per book.* I understand that accepting the 2 free books and gifts places me under no obligation to buy anything. I can always return a shipment and cancel at any time. Even if I never buy another book, the two free books and gifts are mine to keep forever.

151/351 HDN E5LS

Name _____ (PLEASE PRINT) _____

Address _____ Apt. # _____

City _____ State/Prov. _____ Zip/Postal Code _____

Signature (if under 18, a parent or guardian must sign) _____

Mail to the Harlequin Reader Service:
IN U.S.A.: P.O. Box 1867, Buffalo, NY 14240-1867
IN CANADA: P.O. Box 609, Fort Erie, Ontario L2A 5X3

Not valid for current subscribers to Harlequin Blaze books.

Want to try two free books from another line?
Call 1-800-873-8635 or visit www.morefreebooks.com.

* Terms and prices subject to change without notice. Prices do not include applicable taxes. N.Y. residents add applicable sales tax. Canadian residents will be charged applicable provincial taxes and GST. Offer not valid in Quebec. This offer is limited to one order per household. All orders subject to approval. Credit or debit balances in a customer's account(s) may be offset by any other outstanding balance owed by or to the customer. Please allow 4 to 6 weeks for delivery. Offer available while quantities last.

Your Privacy: Harlequin Books is committed to protecting your privacy. Our Privacy Policy is available online at www.eHarlequin.com or upon request from the Reader Service. From time to time we make our lists of customers available to reputable third parties who may have a product or service of interest to you. If you would prefer we not share your name and address, please check here. ☐

Help us get it right—We strive for accurate, respectful and relevant communications. To clarify or modify your communication preferences, visit us at www.ReaderService.com/consumerschoice.

HB10R

HARLEQUIN®

A Romance

FOR EVERY MOOD™

Spotlight on

Inspirational

Wholesome romances
that touch the heart and soul.

See the next page
to enjoy a sneak peek from
the Love Inspired® Suspense
inspirational series.

*See below for a sneak peek from
our inspirational line, Love Inspired® Suspense*

*Enjoy this heart-stopping excerpt from
RUNNING BLIND
by top author Shirlee McCoy,
available November 2010!*

*The mission trip to Mexico was supposed to be an
adventure. But the thrill turns sour when Jenna Dougherty
and her roommate Magdalena are kidnapped.*

"It's okay. I'm here to help." The voice was as deep as the darkness, but Jenna Dougherty didn't believe the lie. She could do nothing but lie still as hands slid down her arms, felt the rope around her wrists.

"I'm going to use a knife to cut you free, Jenna. Hold still."

The cold blade of a knife pressed close to her head before her gag fell away.

"I—" she started, but her mouth was dry, and she could do nothing but suck in air.

"Shhh. Whatever needs to be said can be said when we're out of here." Nick spoke quietly, his hand gentle on her cheek. There and gone as he sliced through the ropes on her wrists and ankles.

He pulled her upright. "Come on. We may be on borrowed time."

"I can't leave my friend," Jenna rasped out.

"There's no one here. Just us."

"She has to be here." Jenna took a step away.

"There's no one here. Let's go before that changes."

"It's dark. Maybe if we find a light…"

"What did you say?"

"We need to turn on the light. I can't leave until I know
that—"

"What can you see, Jenna?"

"Nothing."

"No shadows? No light?"

"No."

"It's broad daylight. There's light spilling in from the
window I climbed in through. You can't see it?"

She went cold at his words.

"I can't see anything."

"You've got a nasty bruise on your forehead. Maybe that
has something to do with it." His fingers traced the tender
flesh on her forehead.

"It doesn't matter *how* it happened. I'm blind!"

*Can Nick help Jenna find her friend or will chasing this
trail have Jenna running blindly again into danger?*

*Find out in RUNNING BLIND, available in
November 2010 only from Love Inspired Suspense.*

SHLISEXP1110

FROM #1 *NEW YORK TIMES*
AND *USA TODAY* BESTSELLING AUTHOR

DEBBIE MACOMBER

Mrs. Miracle on 34th Street...

This Christmas, Emily Merkle (just call her Mrs. Miracle)
is working in the toy department at Finley's, the last
family-owned department store in Manhattan.

Her boss (who happens to be the owner's son) has placed
an order for a large number of high-priced robots, which
he hopes will give the business a much-needed boost. In
fact, Jake Finley's counting on it.

Holly Larson is counting on that robot, too. She's been
looking after her eight-year-old nephew, Gabe, ever since
her widowed brother was deployed overseas. Holly plans
to buy Gabe a robot—which she can't afford—because
she's determined to make Christmas special.

But this Christmas will be different—thanks to Mrs.
Miracle. Next to bringing children joy, her favorite activity
is giving romance a nudge. Fortunately, Jake and Holly
are receptive to her "hints." And thanks to Mrs. Miracle,
Christmas takes on new meaning for Jake. For all of them!

Call Me Mrs. Miracle

Available wherever books are sold
September 28!

MIRA®

www.MIRABooks.com

MDM2819